Praise for A Doula's J[...]

'This is not just a Doula['...]
human. The reader is drawn into the complexity of birth with
an energy that mirrors the labour process itself.

Hazel Tree weaves a web of connectedness: of emotions,
sensations and bodily functions; of relationships between
birthing partners; of the link between birth and personal
identity; of mutual support in a community and of our
affinity with the elements and seasons of the natural world.
The fast-paced style blends the spiritual and the practical,
drama and reflection, humour and pain. Prepare to laugh and
cry and to learn something about yourself.'

-Jill Treseder,
personal development coach, novelist and author of *'The
Wise Woman Within: Spirals to Wholeness'*
a personal development handbook for women.

'A Doula's Journey is an accurate peek into how one decides
to walk the doula path, and how life goes from there. Hazel
Tree writes with conviction and gives the reader a glimpse
into the life of a doula, the trials and challenges and the joys
that make the life and profession worth-while.

As the Director of Birth Arts International I personally
think all students should read this book and learn from it and
know they are not alone in their working experiences. Birth
is natural and as human beings it works. We are still here
and still having babies since the beginning of time. What is
now missing is the presence of the educated support that
sisters, mothers and aunts used to provide. A doula can help
to fill that role that has been missing for too long.'

-Demetria Clark,
author of *'Herbal Healing for Children.'* Director of *Birth
Arts International* www.birtharts.com
and *Heart of Herbs Herbal School* www.heartofherbs.com

A Doula's Journey

~ A novel ~

∞

Hazel Tree

Published by FeedARead.com Publishing
- Arts Council funded
Copyright 2012 ©Hazel Tree

A CIP catalogue record for this title is available from the British Library

Cover Illustration by Jenny Rose
Email: foxtroternest@yahoo.co.uk

Contents

~

For Rio ~ your birth was my inspiration

~

'Studies have shown that when doulas attend birth, labours are shorter with fewer complications, babies are healthier and they breastfeed more easily.'

-DONA International
www.dona.org

'We learn intensely during our experiences in the womb, during birth and the early hours, weeks and months of our lives. Our earliest experiences imprint and become our subconscious programming. Not only are we building the foundations of a health body, but we also are building the foundation of healthy emotions, response patterns to life, and foundations of healthy relationships.

These established patterns are at the root of many health, relationship, emotional, psychological and learning problems seen at all ages.'

-Wendy Anne McCarty, PhD, RN
Diplomate Comprehensive Energy Psychology
www.wondrousbeginnings.com

~ Author's Introduction ~

Ask any mother about the birth of their child and the chances are that she will remember the event with such clarity that other memories pale in comparison. Giving birth is a transformational event. It is a benchmark in a woman's life and can also profoundly affect the father-to be.

It was not until after I had given birth to my son, and later attended two births of close friends in Guatemala, that it really dawned on me the wide spectrum of birth experiences. Giving birth is an event etched into who we are. But so much about how children are born goes unspoken. I was witness to how the external and internal environment makes a difference in the whole birth experience.

It was through investigations into Midwifery training that I first came across the word Doula. It intrigued me as I rolled the word around my mouth like a boiled sweet. The *Doo-* pouting my lips like I was blowing a kiss to a loved one, followed by the *–la* like a clear note sung in an alpine meadow. I loved that word and clung to it in the sea of medical terminology surrounding the UK culture of birth I had returned to. The *Doo-* and the *-la* led me through an intensive nine month long Holistic Doula preparation course. It was as much a personal journey of discovery as a preparation to support women during their birthing year. I felt honoured to be working with the energy that surrounds birth. I found it is not only transformational for the family involved but also for those around them. I saw how the personal and professional paths of those working with this energy intertwined in a unique way. It was hard to separate them. Being a Doula is not just a job, it is a life path, a calling. I wanted to do justice to the incredible personal growth that can happen when someone embraces their life calling.

Writing a story that intertwined fictional characters and events, with information and scientific theory (and a generous handful of horticulture for good measure), as well as spiritual path and personal healing was like weaving a rich tapestry. By writing fiction I found the freedom I was looking for to share some of the dance, and journey of what it can be like to become a Doula

This book has given me many gifts in its writing. I feel more connected to the linage of mothers stretching back to the beginning of time. And also excited about the future of humanity as more consciousness is being brought to how our babies are being born. My hope is that this book will go out into the world and share the message of celebrating childbirth as a unique transformational journey, which can be enriched by the presence of a Doula as birth companion to the birthing family.

Hazel Tree

~ Foreword ~

Our culture of birth in the Western World has become increasingly medicalised and we are now in a position where childbirth involving technological interventions and a menu of drugs has become the norm. Directly challenging this, there is a worldwide movement of Doulas and Midwives who are speaking out for natural birth, calling for women to claim back their birth rights, to empower themselves to take responsibility for their own experiences of birth. In seeing birth as a natural, awe-inspiring process rather than as a necessary evil to endure, we can transform not only the experiences of women giving birth but also the experiences of babies being born. The role of the birth attendant is instrumental in challenging attitudes and enhancing birthing experiences for mothers, fathers and babies alike. In this way, the Doula is part of a universal force which has the potential to change the world.

As a birth worker, I co-run the Exeter Homebirth Group and work with many families in this capacity, offering support and a listening ear. Working with women and their families as they prepare for the arrival of a baby is a great honour and it is always a time of great learning. My own year-long training to become a Doula was an intensive and enriching experience, connecting with other women as well as with the female wisdom of the Ages.

Hazel Tree's novel reveals a tale of discovery, exploring the nature of birth and the essence of womanhood. As a Doula, Mother and supporter of women in many voluntary capacities, Hazel has long been drawn to work with birth and the great power it holds. Her expression of that passion throughout this text is bold, informed and rich with meaning. In bringing together her own years of birth work with her knowledge and the experiences of those she works and shares her life with, she has created an essential read for anyone drawn to work with birth or to learn more about the development of the female role in our culture.

A Doula has a privileged position, welcoming new life into the world. The learning process involved in becoming a Doula creates a universal connection with women.

Hazel's flowing feminine style and soulful imagery make this novel a very special and beautiful journey for its readers as well as the characters within it. As the narrator, Joy, takes a three month journey to begin her journey as a Doula, she also explores her passions as an Artist and begins to understand her own troubled arrival into a broken family. The impact of the truths she unearths and the way in which this allows her to work with families is profound, the beginnings of her newfound quest for understanding and personal growth.

In her novel, Hazel connects with the deeply rooted misconceptions and problems our society has created for birth and seeks a primal connection with the ancient wisdom from which positive birthing experiences are created.

Having become increasingly distanced from her origins, Joy begins her reconnection with her roots by embracing the natural world and becoming part of something larger than herself. This leads her to explore the world of birth and launches her on a journey of self-discovery and connections with other women in her community.

The new friendships and opportunities that arise for Joy offer sources of inspiration, development and learning that are relevant to all of us as we move through our lives within a society that is often unable to nurture us on every level. Engaging with and reflecting upon the themes of this novel can lead us all to consider the impact of our own contribution to the world and take steps towards a more fulfilling lifestyle.

This is not just a book for Doulas; it is a book for women.

Claire Arnold
www.writingwaves.wordpress.com
Doula, Mother and Writer in Devon

A Doula's Journey

~ Prologue ~

My name is Joy. As a child my name felt heavy. I wanted to become ordinary, to be able to melt into a crowd. But I always stood out. I couldn't help it. I was tall and my hair was like a beacon calling for attention. I didn't like my name. I couldn't identify with it. The lightness that surrounded the word and the feeling of celebration seemed to tease me. My name followed me around like a shadow. All my life I had been asking myself, 'What is Joy?' But nothing prepared me for when I finally experienced it. It was unlike anything I could have imagined. But I'm getting ahead of myself. Often we need to go back in order to understand where we are and where we are going.

These pages are the daily musings of my journal. My life has not been an easy one. It's been complicated. Yet writing down this inner world seems to help keep things in order, like a trail of breadcrumbs while I wander off into a dark forest that is full of hungry wolves. Maybe the breadcrumbs will help me find my way out again or maybe they will just help to curb the appetite of the wolves I see out of the corner of my eye. I don't have a map. Maybe someone else does, but who could possibly know where it is I have to go in order to recover those parts of me that are lost?

Feeling incomplete became natural for me while I was growing up, like living without an arm. But I somehow found a way to carry on despite the inner wounds. Other senses came to compensate for that huge empty hole that threatened to consume me should I look too long into its depths. I learnt to run. I learnt not to ask too many questions. I learnt that knowledge can be a dangerous thing in the wrong hands and that survival meant keeping my head down. I kept watching out of the corner of my eye in order to make sure those wolves didn't come too close. That was long ago now.

There did come a time in my life when everything was alright. This happiness crept up on me and it felt good. It felt like I knew what I was doing. Life had a purpose bigger than just my own personal needs. It all started with the birth of a baby. I lived alone and babies were the last thing on my mind as I sat in the studio overlooking the crashing waves of the sea. In the studio I used the past as fuel to create works of art. My parents had given me something to work from, a deep well of emotions that could be wielded like a sword to carve out my creativity. I could either wield it or be cut to shreds. So I developed the capacity to delve deep into myself and fish out creativity like the fisherman I watched working from their boats. The baby was my best friend's and the feeling I experienced was light and buoyant. But it wasn't joy. My happiness was bound to pleasure and the need for positive reward.

My shadows still felt heavy and cumbersome. How could I have thought that after that I could be a Doula and help people transition into life as a family when my own story was such a mess? I felt like a fraud pretending that I knew what a healthy family was like.

My father was absent from the moment I arrived in the world. He left without a backward glance. Did he even look at me once? What did I do in those first minutes of life to cause such a thing to happen?

Mother says my father died crossing the road. That's when she's feeling exceptionally cheerful. At other times I remember hearing the stories of him being a sailor who had a wife in every port or a criminal on the run from the law. Depending on what she was drinking, a different story might slide out of her mouth, sneaking its way past the cigarette constantly sealed in her lips to hit me full force in the chest. In time I learnt to duck and the story would sail past me to disappear into the ether along with the thousands of other lies thrown in my direction.

Truth was not a word I knew until I was twelve and Grandpa told me, 'The truth my girl, is that without green plants, life on earth just wouldn't be here.'

That was before he was found clutching his heart, belly up on the ground among the plants he loved so much.

'Truth Grandpa, what's that?' The innocence of my question still strikes me. What is truth? I know now that it is different for different people. But he spoke of simple truths, of food chains and sunlight, of rainfall and soil composition. We didn't really go in for philosophical discussion about the essential nature of truth. We talked about plants.

So my journal begins the day it all happened, the day I held a new-born baby in my arms. She was just seconds old and made me realize that maybe there was more to life than painting. Little did I know then how that tiny babe would begin a chain reaction that would set my whole world on fire. How the old demons were there, lurking beneath the apparently calm surface waiting for such an opportunity as this to emerge and let it rip. With so many unanswered questions there was only so long that I could ignore the gnawing sensations and set out to look for answers.

Deep inside me I knew that there must be another way, a way to heal my past in order to move on with my life. I wanted to be happy. I wanted to make others happy as well. It is a beautiful world that we live in. I looked out of my window and saw the sun reflecting off the blue sea like a thousand jewels and felt the light in my heart waiting to be set free. I just wasn't sure how to make this happen, how to be freed from my own cage. This is my story of freedom.

~ February ~

Sunday 14th February

Today was an incredible day. I know that my life will never be the same. Something changed inside me today, like a curtain opening to reveal the landscape outside the room I had been locked into for years.

I wasn't supposed to be at her birth. I'd tagged along to a couple of antenatal classes when Nick couldn't make it but I wasn't part of the birth plan. I was simply going to prepare the welcome home feast after the birth.

But when I went over to my friend Jelly's to drop off the bits of shopping I had picked up that morning, there Jelly was, puffing like a train. She opened the door cheeks red, eyes wild and focused on some place a mile behind me.

'Got to go,' she said and scuttled upstairs clutching her huge belly. We'd been friends for so long I just went inside wondering what on earth was going on. I knew the pregnancy made her eat strange foods and thought she was rushing to the bathroom. I put the kettle on and waited to hear the toilet flush. But it didn't.

Instead I heard strange grunting sounds coming from upstairs.

'Angelica!' I shouted, using her full name for maximum effect. But there was no answer. When I went up, the bathroom door was open and she was half naked and straining. I caught my breath. She looked up at me and said the words in a whisper.

'The baby is coming.'

What! Now? The baby wasn't due for a week and her husband Nick was away on a shoot. Thoughts flashed through my mind. Should I call an ambulance? Taxi? Doctor? But then time seemed to stop. I could hear the blood pumping in my ears and my breath caught in my throat. Jelly was holding the baby's head in her hands as it stuck out between her legs. I remember seeing the baby's dark wet hair. Jelly slowly looked up and simply said, 'Get a towel.'

Everything slowed down from that point. I was super aware of my hands catching the baby as it slid out. Time seemed different. It bent, stretched and defied all laws of physics. I looked down and there she was, a little baby girl lying in my arms. She was still wet from the watery womb. But she was wide awake, looking right at me. I looked back, amazed at what I was holding. She was so perfect. It seemed like an eternity passed. When I looked up at Jelly she was leaning back on the toilet breathing deeply, eyes closed. I looked back at the baby.

'Hello,' I said. I gently wrapped her in the towel I had grabbed and tried to pass her to the waiting arms of her mum.

The midwife arrived soon afterwards and was shocked by what had happened.

Right after the birth I had gone downstairs to phone the midwifery team and tell them we had a baby. But my mobile phone was out of credit. I couldn't even find Jelly's phone and the home phone was temporarily out of order. Jelly was shouting at me from the bathroom to come back quickly.

'I'm going to drop her,' she shouted. I took the stairs two at a time racing back. The main problem was that the umbilical cord was really short. The baby was balanced on Jelly's legs as she sat on the toilet. But this was made into an even bigger problem because Jelly felt faint and needed to lie down. We didn't know how long it would take for the placenta to come out.

'Just cut the umbilical cord,' Jelly demanded.

'What?'

'You cut the cord. I need to lie down for a minute then I'll remember where my phone is.'

Maybe neither of us was thinking straight at that moment. The birth happening so quickly had been a shock. Looking back I could have run next door to borrow their phone, but maybe they worked all day. I could have gone to the shop, but that was ten minutes away. I couldn't leave Jelly—not even for a minute.

'Cut it or I'll have to bite through it.' She was getting desperate and looked like a wild animal. Her legs were shaking and it looked like she might fall over if she didn't lie down soon. She had gone quite pale. I felt afraid of her but also of what she was asking me to do.

When she arrived, the midwife took one look at my dental floss umbilical cord wrap and asked in a strange tone, 'What gave you this idea?'

I explained to her how I had needed something to tie the cord before we cut it and the dental floss had been right there. It also seemed like the cleanest thing I could get my hands on. We'd used a fresh razor blade of Nick's to do the actual cutting of that thick curly cord, breaking the nine months connection between mother and baby. The midwife smiled and said it actually wasn't such a bad idea, even though it wasn't exactly standard procedure. She poked the placenta around and checked Jelly and the baby girl. She said that her good birth could mean a good life ahead of her.

Then she turned around to me and asked if I was a Doula.

'A what?' I explained that I was a friend of Jelly's, that I was an artist, and had never heard of Doulas. She just smiled. Her smile stuck in my head, it was like there was more to be said but that now wasn't the time. There was a baby in the room.

The baby girl was weighed and measured, and then all the necessary paperwork was completed. She attempted to find the breast, her head bobbing around. Her mouth seemed almost too small to latch on to the big nipple. The midwife gave lots of suggestions and finally baby was happily sucking away.

I went home briefly to pick up some pyjamas, a toothbrush and my journal before going back. I tucked myself up in the spare room with my hot water bottle while Jelly and her baby were fast asleep in the room next door.

Nick will be back first thing but they spent most of the evening on Skype so it's almost like he's been around already in a funny kind of cyberspace way.

It took an hour to get the whole story from Jelly. It's not every day that someone has a baby while sitting on the toilet. She wasn't due for another week which is why Nick had gone out of town for a night. The midwife told us, however, that only two per cent of babies are actually born on the projected birth date. The exception, of course, is a scheduled C-section. But everyone had told stories that first babies take forever and Jelly had promised to call Nick the minute anything happened. As it was she didn't have time to do anything. I'm glad I rang the doorbell when I did. Ten minutes later and she wouldn't have answered.

Jelly said it was the weirdest thing because all morning she had been getting these cramps, wondering if it was the curry she had the night before. She didn't even know she was in labour, which I found strange. She described the blood and mucus that she'd found in her underwear when she went to the toilet in the morning, just after Nick left for the train. I really didn't need to hear this but now I was past caring.

It was as though we entered a different dimension. Basic bodily functions became clues, signposts that pointed the way to decipher what had happened. Her body had become an unknown landscape that needed decoding like a forgotten language. And unlike the midwife, Jelly didn't have the knowledge to decipher the clues. The midwife was adept—she could read the signs and use her hands as eyes to feel her way past skin to the invisible world beneath. But the midwife had not been there to tell her that her body was preparing to deliver a child into the world.

Why didn't she call Nick? She said she didn't call him as his work trip was very important and she didn't want him to return for a false alarm. After all, first labours always take forever, don't they?

Just before I rang the bell Jelly had been on the phone to the midwifery team telling them about her period like cramps. They calmed her down and said she probably wasn't in labour but she should stay in touch. Who could have guessed how close she really was to giving birth?

Jelly said she honestly thought she just needed the toilet until she got upstairs and could feel the hair of her daughter's head crowning. The look I caught in her eyes when I had walked into the bathroom captured all the strong emotions ripping through her body. It was a sudden awareness that her body had done something without her knowing. Her body had birthed that baby while her mind had been elsewhere. I have read newspaper stories about women who have given birth while being in a coma. Sometimes the doctors decided to perform a caesarean section on them. But there were dangers because of the risks of anaesthesia and the healing difficulties post-partum. Vaginal birth during a coma was sometimes induced using medications but not always. The unconscious woman's body could birth her baby.

But Jelly wasn't in a coma. She had been doing the dishes moments before. Her body and the baby had decided it was time; they just neglected to inform her. Perhaps her mind didn't need to know.

The phenomenon of painless labour has been known to happen, women like Jelly giving birth during normal daytime activities. But it is so unusual. Who would have thought it could happen to my best friend.

I wonder what she had been thinking about that morning while her body laboured to push her baby down the birth canal. Spiralling round the pelvic bones in that intricate dance that only the body knows, a baby girl emerged into this world of air and light. Into my hands, the very same that write these words. These hands that have nurtured seeds to life through the mediums of soil and water. These hands that bring life to plain white canvas through streaks of colour and form. These hands that have held my head as I cried over my past. These hands of mine that have never known what it is like to hold my father's or mother's hands. My mother didn't like to look at me, let alone touch me. Her touch when it came was cruel and best avoided.

These hands of mine held new life today and I look at them now, turning them over in wonder. They touched something untouched by human hand. My hands were the very first thing that baby felt after leaving her mother's body. How did they feel to her? Were they rough from all the gardening at my allotment? Were they warm or cold? Were they welcome after the womb?

Jelly sighed and lay back on her bed of pillows having come to the bit of the story when I arrived in the bathroom. She looked tired, more tired than I had ever seen her. Dark circles hung around her eyes, but her mouth was smiling.

'But what about all that screaming and rushing to the hospital that always happens on the television?' I asked the midwife. It's not always like that, she said. Sally was her name. I liked her after I stopped feeling intimidated. She was really down-to-earth with a wholesome goodness about her that made me feel at home. Though I could also see there would be no messing with her; she held authority in her bearing. Her manner was no-nonsense and practical.

Jelly looks fine now, totally calm about the whole thing, smiling and making loving noises at the baby, who has yet to be named. But something tells me that everything is not quite right. Maybe it is just me, seeing my old friend in the new light of motherhood. I don't know; I just can't put my finger on it. Something feels odd, out of place.

The baby was crying when I came back from getting my things. Jelly was trying to get baby's little mouth onto her large nipple but the baby kept pulling away and waving her arms around like a windmill.

'I'm doing everything the midwife told me to do,' Jelly exclaimed. 'Why isn't it working?'

I took the baby while she rearranged her throne of cushions on the bed. After a couple more tries the baby eventually gave up and fell asleep. I can imagine it would be tiring after making such a journey into life.

I phoned Jelly's mum, to tell her the news. She was really excited and needed to change her flight dates. She had planned to be there for the birth and despite the surprise I could hear the relief in her voice when I told her everything was fine.

This was an incredible day, one I shall never forget. I love what I do in the studio but have felt like I wanted more human connection, something more. Maybe becoming a Doula, whatever it is, deserves investigation.

Monday 15th February

Nick was gloriously reunited with his now larger family early this morning. He arrived spectacularly, with armfuls of fresh flowers after a stop at the florists on the way back from the train station. He made me tell the story over and over in the car asking all kinds of questions. He laughed till he cried about the dental floss and razor blade. He bounced out of the car the minute I pulled up outside the house. I left them to their reunion upstairs, preferring to stay in the kitchen and get stuck into the piles of dishes and baskets of washing that had amounted over the past twenty four hours. Feeling a bit like an unpaid maid, I wondered when her mother would be arriving.

Actually it felt good to be able to help them out. They snuggled upstairs and didn't have to think about dishes or anything other than being with that pink little bundle wrapped up warmly. It didn't feel right to leave. Later on they both thanked me for doing the dishes and I could see they were also silently thanking me for giving them the space they needed. I heard the baby crying from the kitchen and wondered when the midwife would be back to help with the breastfeeding.

I eventually left and am now wrapped up at home. I just looked back in the journal and read what the midwife had asked about being a Doula. I am wondering what that queer feeling is that I have in the bottom of my stomach. Like butterflies having a party. Actually I'm almost trembling, it's so strange. Could I really become a Doula? Could I become a trained birth attendant to support women during childbirth and witness more of the miracle of birth? My toes are curling and it all feels quite extraordinary. I never thought about it before but it feels quite profound, like there has been a voice talking in the background and I never paid it much attention before. I don't know, maybe I'm just over-tired and excited. I'll wake up tomorrow and this will all be like a dream.

After the birth last night I only slept in snatches, waking at every snuffle and movement from the other room. It felt like I was on duty somehow. I went in a couple of times but felt awkward and didn't know what to do.

I also keep going over and over what happened yesterday. I remember so clearly how the baby just landed in my hands, this little being with perfect fingers and toes. What a feeling, what emotion, what life raw and beating in the palm of my hand. I didn't notice a bit of fatigue as I leapt out of bed this morning. I bounced around cuddling the baby while Jelly showered and changed, feeling like I could do this every day. I feel like a new world has opened its door to me. I am both afraid and excited. Was this how Alice felt when she entered wonderland?

Tuesday 16th February

They have called her Valentina—being a valentine birth and bringing such love with her into the world. Quite a name to live up to, I thought to myself. Will she go around breaking hearts or making matches?

I went over to see them this morning. Jelly's mum had arrived and stationed herself in the kitchen, making tea and keeping the house in order. The midwife was upstairs when I arrived and I didn't want to intrude. Everyone in the house was beaming and telling Jelly what a miracle woman she was to give birth like that and how amazing her body was. She was still looking tired and the smile almost looked painted on now. I didn't say anything, not wanting to break the spell.

The baby looks so angelic when she finally falls asleep. Huge silly smiles hang off Nick's face as he lolls around, very happy for Jelly's mum to wait on him, mother and babe while the new mother is half naked, propped up in bed.

'All those years of topless sunbathing finally come in useful,' she said with a wry grin. Little Valentina is tucked up next to her in the bed. They decided they couldn't put her in the nursery. They have their argument ready: the World Health Organisation recommends sharing a room for the first six months. Luckily their bed is big enough for half the neighbourhood to fit in, let alone a small baby. I wondered why that was recommended. Nick said he had read that a newborn can forget to breathe unless there are other people in the same room. Or perhaps it was about the carbon dioxide balance in the air. I forget.

Nick is also taking his role of official photographer very seriously. As he missed the birth, he is making up for it with hundreds of shots of tiny feet, fingers, curled ears and frog like legs. He has an amazing eye for seeing through the camera lens. That's why his business is doing so well and he gets requested to do photo shoots far away. He excels at what he does; it is an art form.

I knew something was up when they sat me down before I left, one on each side. They asked me if I would do them the honour of becoming Valentina's godmother (fairy god-mother, Jelly said).

'If I would do you the honour,' I stuttered. 'It would be me who would be honoured.' It was settled and I felt even more a part of the new extended family.

After that I took the dog for a long walk along the beach. He needed it as much as I did. No one else was going to be leaving that house today. Grandma is on phone patrol. Dad is behind the camera. Jelly is on the cushion throne and the baby in the middle. The walk was cold. February winds and dramatic crashing waves against a backdrop of a fierce thundery sky made me feel alive, surrounded by the raw elements.

I realized how being with the Blake family (it's not just Jelly and Nick now) has made me feel useful and given me a role that I happily slipped into. I felt peaceful and like I had a purpose for the first time in a long while.

These past months have been wrenching and lonely. Getting lost in my studio has been therapeutic and there has been some good art work come out of it. But I want some life again. Some raw life, contact with real living people, not just paintings and sketches. And something more than day to day human contact. I have good people in my life these days, friends and neighbours that listen and share. I have a lot to be grateful for. It hasn't always been gratefulness I've felt, especially after Byron left. Aside from that I can't even begin to unravel my childhood scars.

But things have moved on, I'm ready for something more now. Not a child of my own. I couldn't face that, not yet. Something about being able to hand the baby back when it's time to go back to my own life really appeals to me. I don't want to give up my freedom or my art, as that is my selfish pleasure and my work. Something is on the cards. The wind seems to whisper it and the gulls in the air seem to call it. I still can't quite hear what it is, not yet. But I feel it. I feel different. I feel alive. I haven't written this much in my journal for a very long time. Instead I have been using paint to express what inner thoughts have been blowing through my mind. But now it's different—something has changed. I'm just not entirely sure what yet.

Wednesday 17th February

My god-daughter (I like the way that sounds) gave me a good, long, hard stare today. It felt like she could look right into the very depth of my being. It was almost unnerving it was so intense. Her crystal clear eyes were like two deep molten pools of sapphire. She looked and looked and looked. In the moment I locked eyes with her, I knew that I was totally in her power. There is nothing I won't do for that child. She has me heart, mind and soul.

What Jelly and Nick must feel is astounding. She is a physical embodiment of their love for each other and holds their very DNA in her cells. They do look like different people now. I still haven't been able to sit down with Jelly and ask what's going on with her. She just doesn't look quite right. I had to leave in the end today. It was like they were on holiday in a place I could look at but was not mine to visit, at least not in exactly the same way. I got a taste of it looking into those sapphire pools.

I came home and googled 'birth attendant', never imagining the 364,000 results that came up. Compare that to the 5,860,000 results when I googled 'Doula.' I never thought there would be so much information out there. How could a worldwide profession exist that I had never even heard of before? I admit my mouth was hanging open while I scrolled through the millions of results. I felt overwhelmed and out of my depth like I knew the sea floor was there but couldn't quite find my footing on it. It felt a bit more stable when I found what is happening locally. Not too far away from where I live is a Doula trainer and somehow seeing a familiar place name made it all feel a bit more real. I felt like I could have been dreaming otherwise. Like I have stumbled into this fairy tale land where women celebrate their rites of passage and are accompanied by their blood sisters during difficult labours. But actually Doulas are both ancient and modern, evolving from something cultural and intuitive to something more organized and professionally trained. The modern day division of the nuclear family can mean that families no longer all live in the same street, town or even country. And close emotional support is often absent in our busy world. This is the gap that well trained Doulas can fill during the highly emotional time surrounding child birth.

I dropped a quick email to this local trainer. Tapping the words out quickly, I explained what had led me to google 'Doula' and how her name had come up. It will be interesting to see what she says, if she replies. Regardless of what happens, it did feel good to share what's happened and to see it in writing on my computer screen.

I have started sowing the first spring seeds up on the allotment. The flat I live in has no outdoor space at all and I treasure having that piece of land to dig, to sow, to grow vegetables and fruit bushes, to watch the apple trees blossom and to sit in my shed among the tools. It is somewhere I can reconnect with Grandpa and use all the knowledge he passed down to me. I often think the allotment is like a slice of pizza, surrounded as it is by similar patches on every side. Other people are planting and harvesting on their own little slices all around me, undivided by roads or walls or fences, just small grass paths marking the boundaries between plots. Some people grow lots of fruit, others like to have ornamental flowers; some like rows of potatoes, others like giant strawberry patches. It is like a giant smorgasbord.

Today I planted summer cabbage seeds, early carrots and a few early peas under cloches to help keep them warm. I hope they survive the journey through the temperamental weather we are having. Last year was cruel and took so many seedlings with a late frost.

After all these weeks of clearing debris and dead plants from the allotment it felt inspiring to hold seeds to new life and growth in my palm, then to commit them to the dark soil with hope for their future. My hands held the possibility of new life, new growth.

Walking through the park later there was a tree full of beautiful blossoms, like upturned goblets. They were white inside and an incredible pink outside. I stood there grinning, feeling grateful for being alive to see that the earth was also coming alive around me.

An elderly lady stopped to chat. Having seen me standing there looking at the blooms, she began to tell me the story behind the park.

She also told me the names of rare trees and shrubs found in the park. The Magnolia, Rhododendrons, Azaleas and the very sought after of exotic flora ~ the Paper Handkerchief tree. These rare shrubs and trees were collected from around the world at the beginning of the twentieth century. A young plant hunter by the name of Ernest Wilson was employed by the famous Vetch brothers to travel to the end of the Earth to bring back viable plant specimens. In those days plant hunting was big business, with thousands of new varieties of plants being introduced into the country.

Standing there in the spring sunshine I realized I had never given a second thought as to where all these plants had come from. It was fascinating stepping back in time to when these gardens were first planted. How did those trees get here?

The elderly lady in the park had found a willing ear and continued sharing the history of where we were standing.

Ernest Wilson fell in love with a young lady and married her in 1902 but had to leave the country just six months later. He would visit exotic lands and bring back specimens he found there, having been sent to find a specific plant or tree and travelling many months and many miles until it had been found. The story goes that his wife, Helen Ganderton, was an avid horticulturist in her own right. He would always find a way to bring her back something special to add to her garden. Her passion for gardening made her wait in eager anticipation for the plants he brought as much as for the man himself. Over the years together they built up a stunning collection of trees, shrubs and plants. I'm sure many must have perished in the cold English winter and wet dull days so far from tropical sunshine. But many survived and are a testimony to the love that plant hunter felt for his lady. Their grand house is now converted into flats, large high ceilinged places, some with views over the park. Even during darkest winter the park holds beauty in its design.

The Handkerchief Tree was bare today; I couldn't imagine why it could be called such a name. When I asked how it had earned that title I was told to wait a while.

Now with spring just around the corner the earth has all the energy of a tightly coiled spring waiting to uncurl and burst into life. It must be infectious because I feel like I could burst being so full of life right now.

Thursday 18th February

Last night I had a dream that was so vividly full of colours and textures. As I slid into waking, the realisation that it was only a dream slowly dawned on me. But it was hard to believe as it seemed so solid, so tangible.

I had moved my home into a huge, old, gnarled tree. It was hollow inside with a massive space in the centre where I could walk around. There were rooms coming off it at right angles. A man was also moving in at the same time and I helped him with his bags. Then someone else came over to help me with my bags. Later it struck me that in this place I needed to do nothing for myself. Everything I did for another person, I literally received for myself. The more I did for other people, the more I received. It was so interesting. The more I gave away, the more I received. The more I helped, the more I was helped. The more I listened, the more I was heard. Now I'm wondering if this is something I need to be more aware of in my own life. I have been self-sufficient all my life. I used to think that accepting help from another person was a sign of weakness. But after investigating yesterday what Doulas do to support others I feel it could be time to re-evaluate that belief. A Doula's work seems to be all about doing things for other people. How can I do that if I cannot be open to receive help myself?

Friday 19th February

So many things have happened today. Different jigsaw pieces that have been sliding around are coming together and beginning to make sense. The most sense they've made in a long time. It makes me wonder if something is about to go horribly wrong, with all this rightness going on.

Externally, a chance meeting, an email thrown out onto the wind of internet explorer and a face in a crowd all seem so random. But they have all connected. It almost feels like a conspiracy to pull me along a pre-designated track, like the path has always been there waiting. Maybe part of me has always known the path was there, but I've never had the courage to look it squarely in the face. It feels as if a silenced part of me has finally been heard and listened to. As I open more fully to hear that new song, my whole soul is singing it and it becomes louder and louder. Could this be a calling? That was what Leanne called it. 'Finding your destiny,' she said. It could be true. I feel the same way about my art ~ when I am in the studio and in the creating zone it is like my soul hums with satisfaction. This is at a different pitch, but from the same note. Leanne is the Doula trainer I wrote to and poured my story out to in black and white. She was so welcoming in her reply that I felt at ease. We spoke on the phone yesterday and then ended up at the same birthday party last night. It was one of those strange coincidences of having mutual friends.

Then this morning I met the midwife Sally at the deli counter. We began chatting over the olives and pesto sauce. She appreciates Doulas and thinks they can bring something special to the birthing room with their continuity of care. Sally commented on how calm and confident I had been at Jelly's birth. I felt my chest swell to be praised by someone so experienced and knowledgeable. Inspiring and inspired. By another coincidence she has an allotment at the same site as mine so we exchanged numbers and plans for seed swapping.

After talking with these two women about being a Doula, I am convinced to walk this path and see where it goes.

Valentina's birth taught me so much, about birth and about myself. Sure, it all happened really fast but it was an incredible experience. Now I realize that there is a road to becoming a Doula and somehow I find myself standing on it. I look back wondering how I came to be here but at the same time looking ahead with excitement about where it is all going.

I am going to be a Doula. I'm still learning what that means but whenever I say it (and I've been repeating it to myself a lot) it's like pinching myself to see if I'm dreaming. But I don't wake up; this is real and becoming more real by the day. There is a Doula training course beginning next month and my name is on the list to begin. I know it's crazy, a few days ago I didn't even know what a Doula was ('a who-la?') and now I'm going to be one. Well, let's start with the training.

To be honest I would happily attend birth for free, which is good because as a trainee Doula I may well do just that. To learn a skill like this, only so much can come from books. It is a hands-on skill that needs to be learnt through direct experience of the senses: eyes, ears, hands and heart as well as academic study.

Saturday 20th February

Another strange thing happened today. I had been looking at a book on the internet about birth and today it was placed in my hand by a friend. It was another of those coincidences that seem to be popping out of the woodwork these days.

The weather today was so fine and bright. The ground at the allotment was just begging to be dug. Many people were there chatting and feeling the joviality of the warmer days.

The whole world seems to be singing, 'We did it. We survived. The darkest days of winter are behind us now.'

The asparagus bed I'm preparing requires such loving care. Every scrap of weed must come out. The double digging brought up interesting treasures from the past ~ like hacksaw blades, a cracked cup and bits of string. It is a modern-day archaeological dig, investigating the lives of the previous generation who drank tea from china cups and repaired all that they could with string and ingenuity. Some wonderfully rich manure from the riding stables seemed to have the ground groaning at receiving this delicious feast of fresh life teeming with nutrients and wriggling delights. They say a good asparagus bed will last for 20 years so I am planting this bed not just for me but for future generations.

How will Valentina be in a year's time? Maybe her little fingers will be squashing steamed asparagus spikes before dunking them in soft boiled eggs. I dig for me and my delight at eating fresh and organic foods. Yet at the same time I dig for the future and now for her, too.

My arms and legs screamed with aches upon returning home until they were soaked in a herbal bath so deep and hot as to quell their persistent moans.

Sunday 21st February

Last night I had a dream about waiting for a train. I was on a platform, much like the one in London near Sophia and John's house. There were hundreds of people waiting there as well. The man in the ticket booth told me the next train would be in fourteen minutes. So I found a space to sit and waited. Exactly fourteen minutes later a bus appeared on the train tracks. The whole crowd stormed up the steps and over the bridge en masse as they started filling up this bus. I turned to the man in the ticket booth, 'You didn't say that it was going to be a bus-train.' For some reason I didn't like buses one bit. Buses that thought they were trains were even less appealing.

'When is the next train?' I demanded. A train was due in another fifteen minutes. I decided to wait rather than join the rugby scrum that was happening on the other platform. The crowd was desperately trying to squeeze into a space much too small for my liking.

A young child sat on the steps looking lost. I went over to her and gently untangled the shoes that, instead of being on her feet, were tied together and hung around her neck. Then I woke up and dawn was on the horizon.

Now I'm sitting here in bed writing this as dawns thin pink rays come slinking in through the window. My room takes on a warm glow. From outside I can hear a bird's song. It is all like a perfectly timed concert ~ lights, camera and action. I feel thankful to be here now, to be able to hear the birds and see the light show of the universe unfolding in front of me.

What could the dream mean? It felt strange and unrelated to anything in my life. I thought about how I had decided not to get on the train because I didn't want to, then found the child sitting by herself and helped to untangle her. Maybe a few months ago I would have gotten onto the train merely because everyone else was doing it. I realized that I now no longer feel like I have to do what everyone else is doing, especially if it is not what I want to do. I felt an affinity with that little girl. Perhaps she is a little me, lost and tangled in her own shoe laces with no-one to help untangle them. I do feel like I am helping myself these days, and maybe I will begin to untangle the mess of my past and free that little girl lost inside me.

Monday 22nd February

Everywhere I go these days I see pregnant women. It's funny because I once would have looked at them with concern, or maybe quiet envy of their swollen bellies and ease of procreation. I now see something else as well. I see a radiant glow as these women do the miraculous ~ create a life. I have a new found desire to stop them and ask how they're feeling, what plans they have for the baby, if they get food cravings, if they've thought about having a Doula.

I can see the baby squeezed in among their mother's internal organs, using the only tools at their disposal to make themselves more room. So bladders get elbowed and stomachs get kicked in their fight for space. More often these days I catch their eye and smile, sometimes we talk, if there's time and space. Sometimes they ask me what I do, probably wondering why I'm so interested in their growing bump. Here I test out my new self-statement, synopsis of self, personal mission statement ~ 'I'm a Doula in training,' I reply. Even though my Doula course hasn't taken place yet I feel this is what I am. What I will grow to be. What I am here to do. More than a job, more than a career, it is a calling to work and I can hardly explain how that feels inside my body. It's as though every cell of my being from scalp to toe tingles with knowingness of my place in the world. At last I feel a sense of deep peace penetrating my life and it spirals around this knowingness. Things that used to make me feel crazy or spark me into angry words now don't seem to affect me, like a duck, the water just rolls off my back.

Tuesday 23rd February

Part of me is glad I don't have children, it would have complicated things. Another part of me aches for a child; thankfully this ache doesn't stay but comes and passes quite quickly. I wonder if it is hormonal rather than rational.

I finally spent the afternoon with Jelly and the baby today. Nick was back at work. I went to keep them company and to see if there was anything she needed. She was still in bed when I arrived, looking tired. I could hear the baby crying as I opened the front door with the spare key. Jelly was just looking at the baby when I walked into the room, not doing much, just looking as the baby cried. I sat down on the edge of the bed.

'Do you want me to hold her for a bit?' I asked gently.

I don't think Jelly had really registered that I'd even entered the room. She handed me the baby, who calmed down straight away. Jelly burst into tears.

'She always does that,' Jelly snuffled. 'As soon as she is with someone else she is quiet and happy. But when I hold her, she cries. I don't think she likes me,' she finished with a wail.

I let her tears roll, let her talk out her heart. All the worries came out with the flood water rolling down her face. She felt like such a bad mother. Breastfeeding was really difficult. The baby cried a lot. Jelly was tired. The birth had happened so quickly she didn't feel like she had the time to prepare to become a mother. Everyone else was so happy, telling her how wonderful it was that she had begun to feel like there was something wrong with her for not feeling the same way.

I began to understand the painted on smile and the dark circles. But I offered no suggestions, just listening and holding the baby. What could I say? That everything was fine? It obviously wasn't fine from where Jelly was sitting. Everything was horrible for her. It felt like anything I might have said would have been patronizing. I did my best to listen and listen well.

Finally when she had quietened down I said, 'You sound very tired.' That set her off crying again.

'Yes, I'm so tired. My thoughts aren't straight,' she mumbled. I offered to take Valentina downstairs for an hour or two so she could sleep. She nodded and I think she was asleep before we left the room. Why had it been so hard for Jelly to admit she needed help and that she felt so bad? The answer would have to wait for now. After two hours of holding Valentina I had to leave for an appointment with the art gallery manager. I promised I would be back soon.

Wednesday 24th February

In last night's dream I was on a beach and saw a group of orca whales. The largest came past first and it was so unexpected that it took my breath away. Then came a smaller one which I saw was a calf. After that, more and more orcas of varying sizes swam slowly past me. They were a whole family group. Their calmness affected me and I was mesmerized by these giant mammals serenely passing so close I could reach out and touch them.

After this dream I woke feeling calm. Then I realized that I, too, am a mammal just like them, that all humans are mammals. We give birth to our young. We feed them milk in their early days to sustain them. The word mammal itself comes from the Latin word 'mamma' meaning breast. Funny how that sounds a lot like what we call our own mothers. I remember reading that all mammals also have a placenta during gestation, that life-giving organ nestled within the womb. Whales must have an enormous placenta compared to humans!

Despite all the trappings of modern day civilisation we are all just mammals; living, breathing, giving birth and creating families. We are part of the web of life, just like the whales and the fish and the birds in the sky. We are also like the whales for we live in family groups. This made me think of my family and also of my community, my friends and neighbours. The people who touch my life every day, the people who stock the shelves of the local shop, the bus drivers and telephone repairers, the unseen companies who keep my utilities working and the road sweepers who keep my street clean. I feel gratefulness to them all, to everyone who is a part of my life. They are all my grand extended family.

After breakfast I took a walk through the park and saw Hilary again, the woman with the dogs who had found me grinning at the magnolia flowers the other day. We sat in the morning sun and shared stories. It was comfortable just sitting and talking. I was surprised to hear myself talking about things I hadn't thought about in a long time ~ where I grew up, childhood dogs and my grandma's flower garden that grandpa kept long after her death. I even found myself sharing some of the dysfunction of my family, memories long left dormant. Hilary is easy to talk to. Her life has been long and varied. I found out that her ancestors were the ones that owned the big house in which she now lives in one of the converted flats. She invited me over one day for coffee, and to see the view of the park from the long sash windows.

The afternoon at the allotment was delightfully filled with crisp air and bright sun. Although the sun still hangs low on the horizon as if too shy to take centre stage in the sky. More digging, a bean trench this time to go around the bamboo wigwam, digging deeply to fill in with the dug-over compost heap from last year. But this was a job done roughly, not with the dedicated finesse required for the asparagus bed.

Thursday 25th February

Today I spent my time in the studio, feeling creative and working hard. I slip into The Presence of Being to create my art. The outside world seems to disappear and the present moment is all there is. I am what I am and for a few blissful hours there is nothing else that matters. I feel at home in this little world I have created, surrounded by my pots of paint and bottles of potions. But something in it has changed slightly, I realized today, as if a new seasoning had been added to a soup. I have the feeling that my life will never be the same as I have known it, whatever may happen.

Friday 26th February

Somehow I have my first client. She surprisingly has appeared in my life, making me feel like this path is becoming more real every day. Although it is still early days and we haven't committed to working together yet. We had a long phone conversation this morning and we felt a connection between us.

Her name is Anne-Marie. She heard about me through someone in the Arts group who I'd been blathering onto about the wonders of Doulas during one of our sessions. Over the oil pastels and charcoals, I'd told my friend Marilyn how a Doula's presence during birth can have a positive effect on the birth outcome. Statistics support the facts that having a Doula at your birth could mean less pain during labour, as well as a fifty per cent reduction in emergency C-section rate and a sixty per cent reduction in unnecessary cuts to the perineum. I distinctly remember telling Marilyn this as she squirmed and crossed her legs, saying something about oranges and lemons. Still, she must have been listening as she told her pregnant friend about how Doulas can help in birthing. The next thing I know, her friend wants me to attend her birth.

This new development is happening so quickly. Am I ready to support another woman during childbirth? Can I really do this? What do I do? With Jelly's birth, I just reached out and the baby plopped into my hands. It was Jelly who did it and was in charge. Or rather, Jelly's body did it.

I still think about those first few minutes in her bathroom. The three of us all looked at one another like party guests that get the dates wrong and arrive a day early ~ 'Surprise!' That had happened to me at Suzie and Mick's one evening. I'd felt so embarrassed but they were lovely and gave me the spare room and a chopping board to help with the preparation for the next day's banquet!

The Doula course begins before Anne-Marie's due date, a whole two weeks before, in fact. If it goes well I shall be a 'real' trainee Doula before her baby is due. After beginning my studies, I need to attend two births and be assessed before I can officially complete the course. I was really glad to hear about all the on-going support I would have while still in training. I'm nervous about making mistakes, and not knowing what to do, among a pile of other concerns and worries that roam around my head.

I'm going over to Anne-Marie's house next week for coffee. On the phone we'd have sounded like two old friends if you'd happened to have been walking by and heard us nattering on. Although there is more I need to learn, I feel good about this, about how it's landed in my lap. I hadn't been searching for a client. It feels like a good sign. I hope it is.

Jelly was really positive about this new development in my Doula journey. We went out to lunch at that little place we love in town. We used to go there often before Valentina made her appearance. It was lovely being there again, the three of us this time. There were cappuccinos for the ladies and mummy's milk for the little princess. We laughed so much I was crying. It was Jelly's first public breastfeeding experience and she was trying to do it discretely. She felt hypersensitive to the judgement of other people in the café. But it was funny at the same time. It was good. She was looking a lot more like herself again but with a new glow around her. She has changed and as I looked at her today, holding Valentina and laughing, I realized how beautiful she is, both inside and out.

Earlier she had told me how just talking with me the other day about how awful she had been feeling really helped. She had felt like such a bad mother for even feeling that way. Sleeping had helped her gain more perspective. I couldn't see what it was that I had done exactly, but she assured me that I had been brilliant. I'd been reading about how many women get these feelings after giving birth. A cocktail of hormones mixed with disrupted sleep patterns and an over-generous dash of preconceived ideas was a heady mix. Some women suffered terribly and these feelings turned into post-natal depression, a horrible mental illness. It seemed like Jelly had managed to let the feelings pass.

The woman who runs the café came over and sat down with us. She told her story of having three kids all under five years old when she was younger and breastfeeding big ones and little ones at the same time in all kinds of places. Her stories were wonderfully down-to-earth and real. We all howled with laughter when she told us about her adventures. After that, Jelly noticeably relaxed even more. She had joined the ranks of motherhood and was not alone in her struggle.

It felt so good to be out together, laughing and blowing away the dark clouds that had been lurking on the horizon.

Saturday 27th February

I had a dawn walk on the beach this morning. The light was incredible and it was amazing to be out in it. I started sketching some ideas to develop later. The waves were the little lapping ones that go plop, plop, plop as they roll onto the sand. Surprisingly, lots of people were out walking early as well and many 'good mornings' were exchanged. I love mornings like this; I feel part of the community.

Later, at home, the sketches quite easily turned into a couple of lovely watercolour paintings on the new paper from Jackson's art suppliers.

The clear light is so inspiring. It makes even simple rock structure and sand turn into something divine. This morning also became experimental ~ I made towers of pebbles and included them in my drawings. Something about them adds a certain quality to the purely natural scenes and speaks to a deeper part of me.

On the beach I had found a lovely smooth pair of stones and when they balanced together they resembled a pregnant woman reclining. The image was so interesting that I took photos to bring back to the studio. I wanted to be able to copy the light and shadows exactly. The photos themselves look amazing on the computer. I spent half the evening trying to use different mediums to get the shape of the pregnant woman just right. But found I was trying too hard when, in fact, just the slightest suggestion of a pregnant body speaks much louder to our anthropomorphic detectors than an over-exaggerated detailed figure. Finally, hours later, I am about to sleep with images of pregnant stones dancing in front of my eyes.

Sunday 28th February

Yesterday's work still looks good to me. We'll see what the gallery owners think about it and whether it sells.

Tomorrow is my first meeting with Anne-Marie. She is keen for us to meet up sooner rather than later as she is already thirty seven weeks pregnant. I'm not really sure how I should prepare for our meeting. I shall have to follow my intuition for the time being as the Doula training course doesn't begin until next weekend. I have already been reading some books from the recommended reading list but it still feels I need to do so much more since there is so much to learn. Childbirth is a massive topic. I guess for now I will simply have to trust that all will be well tomorrow.

'All will be well
And all will be well
And all manner of things will be well.'

I sang these words in the studio all evening after hearing them on the radio. How can radio waves travel so easily through the walls of my house when the mobile phone signals have so much difficulty? I have to either stand on the back step or hang out of a window to get a phone signal. But the radio will happily sing its tunes from anywhere upstairs or downstairs. I shall let this song sing in my head and wait to see what tomorrow will bring.

~ March ~

Monday 1st March

This morning I met Anne-Marie. I drove to her house which is in a tiny village not five miles from my town. It is along a single track lane with grass growing up the middle, like entering another world. Tall hedges on either side made it feel I was driving through a green tunnel to emerge on the other side, ejected onto a gravel driveway. An avenue of trees marched up either side of the driveway leading up to the big grey stone house with wooden lintels.

I remember my thoughts at that stage were self-doubting, wondering if I was imagining all this. I was feeling a bit like I was in a theatre production but someone had forgotten to give me my lines or offer stage direction. I had no idea what to do, so what could I do but be natural and be myself? There were no lines to read, no part to play, no one had told me how to do this or what protocol to follow. I was just a woman meeting a woman, being with women ~ isn't that what the original definition of a midwife was, anyway?

Within minutes of meeting Anne-Marie I was at ease. She hugged me and told me how happy she was that I was there. I realized I didn't have to *do* anything or *be* anyone. Simply being myself and being there with her was enough for now.

We sat in her gorgeous front room with a positively indulgent array of patisserie laid out before us. I confessed my current lack of professional qualifications, explaining about the upcoming course and interesting timing of her call.

Anne-Marie is not a person to worry about details. She was so grateful to have someone to talk to about the baby that she waved my concerns aside with a flick of her fingers and a little 'ffp'. Her husband was Mr Big in the marketing world. Being very busy meant he was hardly around. He had set her up in this fairy tale castle with cleaners, a cook, horses out back and dogs in front of the fire. It felt like I'd stepped into an edition of Home and Country magazine. It all looked so perfect.

Despite the appearance of ease at living such a luxurious life, Anne-Marie confided in me quite quickly that she wasn't born into such luxuries. The speed at which she disclosed this was meant, I think, to set me at ease. Knowing that perhaps we were both playing roles we hadn't always been accustomed to was comforting.

We moved on to talk about her pregnancy: Thirty seven weeks, currently LOA. I had to come home and do some research on baby positions after this. Left Occiput which is the knobbly bit on the back of baby's head, Anterior meaning it is pointing to the front of mum's belly. The midwife had said this was the perfect position for giving birth when she did her house call last Friday. I said nothing, but hadn't been aware that midwives had time to do antenatal house visits.

She'd had no sickness apart from the first month or so, which had the cook pulling her hair out trying to find something that Anne-Marie could keep down. Then she found that plain rice flour pasta was a winner. The sickness slowly passed and now her diet is healthy. Actually, it's amazing! To tell the truth she is glowing with motherhood; her skin is clear, eyes bright, hair shiny and full, swollen belly. She looks the picture of health.

I heard how the routine anomaly scan had come back showing everything as normal. But Anne-Marie had not been satisfied with the results so had discreetly gone to a private doctor to have more tests. These results had also come back all clear. It came across that Anne-Marie was quite a nervous person, and her husband allowed her to do almost anything she wanted. We talked about the many tests she had had performed. She was obviously very happy to be pregnant and yet quite anxious as well.

I got a feeling that there was something she wasn't saying. It felt like she was holding something back and all the other chatter was to cover the fact that she wasn't saying it, whatever it was. Almost like there was an elephant on the table but neither of us chose to mention it. I don't know. Maybe I am imagining it. Maybe it's really none of my business. After all, I'm only the Doula.

We talked a lot about the birth plan, after a delicious lunch which had me wishing I could afford her cook. Anne-Marie had written the plan weeks ago and was keen to share it with me. She'd obviously thought about it a lot. She wanted a natural birth in the midwifery-led unit that was attached to the hospital. She was worried about emergencies during the birth. But she also wanted the freedom to move around in labour and liked the look of the non-traditional space.

She was putting her trust in the medical professionals to inform her if anything wasn't going well and help her make an informed decision. Her husband's job was to be with her at all times. That bit was underlined twice and I got the feeling that maybe Larry wasn't around much due to a busy work schedule. This seemed to be Anne-Marie's way of making sure he was present.

My role hadn't been written in yet. It had only been a few days since she'd heard about me from Marilyn, her weekly veggie box supplier. They had chatted about her pregnancy over the organic cabbage and spuds. The conversation had turned to Doulas and the rest, as they say, is 'her-story'.

Her idea was that my role would be to 'enhance her birth experience.' I'm quoting Anne-Marie. My mind whirled about how I could do this but I didn't have to worry. She had already written down a list of things for me to do. I was to help carry things from the car into the delivery suite. I would assist in arranging the room with pillows and the birth ball as well as aesthetic things like fresh flowers and pictures. I could offer drinks to both her and Larry. There would be sports drinks for Anne-Marie (using the bendy straw) and coffee for Larry (milk with one sugar). She was very precise. I could also offer them the snacks in the ready-packed bag.

I could play some appropriate music during labour. There was a playlist on the iPod for me to copy. At the moment of birth I was to make sure the special birth song she'd chosen was playing. If the need for medical intervention arose she wrote that I was to help them to know their options. I wasn't sure about this one as I am not an expert in medical interventions. But Anne-Marie just smiled and said we'd have to trust the medical professionals. That was what she had planned on doing anyway but had put that in the plan as that is what her Doula guide book suggested she include.

'But,' she reasoned, 'how could you really know better than the medical professionals what interventions I would need?'

I did wonder at this point what else she had put into the birth plan and wasn't really planning on doing.

Mid-afternoon saw me driving away from Little Hengelwook, the castle in the woods, after a four-hour visit. I felt exhausted from concentrating for so long, trying to soak up everything that was going on. She was grateful to have found me, saying that my presence 'felt like the icing on the cake of my perfect birth plan.' I just felt tired and wondered about that elephant neither of us had mentioned.

I'm going back next week to have another morning of coffee and patisserie. That will be after my training weekend so I'm sure there will be many other things for us to talk about. Anne-Marie is so organized that I am sure that she is tapping away on the keyboard right at this minute, inserting the new additions to her five-page birth plan to involve the presence of her Doula ~ me.

The baby's room looked beautiful, already fully stocked with toys, nappies and clothes. Coming back to my small flat felt like walking into a box after the spaciousness of her castle. I felt deflated. How could she have all of that when I have had to struggle to have just a little?

Then I looked out of my window, the light blue painted wooden frame matched the rolling waves of the sea. The sun was going down over the horizon, creating a pink and orange light show across the clouds. My heart lifted as I watched the seagulls soaring along the air currents and I realized just how much I have. I opened the window so I could hear the seagull's throaty cries and the crashing of the waves. The wind whistled through my hair. I couldn't resist throwing on a coat for a quick walk along the beach. The freedom was exhilarating and I could have whooped with the happy feelings of freedom and space swelling my heart. I have it all right here.

Tuesday 2nd March

It was a day in the studio again. The big piece of art is coming along. I added a few of the gulls from last night's flight, their black silhouettes caught against the crashing sea. The greeting card range has been selling well. I will make more when I find some time.

Mum phoned today for the first time in ages. How long has it really been...five months or more? She wasn't at all impressed by my interest in becoming a Doula.

'Why on earth would you want to be involved in that bloody stuff?' Her scathing tone cut through me, grating like fingernails on a blackboard. I remembered just why I'd stopped returning her calls. Last Christmas came and went with only cards passing each other in the post. There is so much criticism and coldness, hurting words and unprovoked attacks. I still have to remember to duck to let those words fly over my head.

Today I told her I had something on the stove and rung off, grateful for the silence that filled my ears when I returned the handset.

I basked in the silence all afternoon, allowing the feelings brought up by hearing her voice to wash through me like the breaking waves of the sea upon the shore. I imagined I was the beach, feeling the strength and unrelenting crash of foam and churning water. I felt the cleansing and washing away of the imprints of harsh words until their image had gone and only a faint memory remained.

The sea also became calmer as the afternoon went on. By sundown it was as flat as a millpond, reflecting the clouds and birds above, still and deep. I walked alone on the beach after the sun had set, enjoying the anonymity of the darkness. It was like a cloak hung over my shoulders and acted as a shroud of silence. There were a few other people around, dog walkers mainly, but I felt the invisibility of the darkness hold me safely. I walked in silence, listening to the rolling waves and the crunching sand under my feet as I allowed the remaining thoughts to roll away.

Wednesday 3rd March

I had a dream last night. I was at some kind of garden fête or summer festival. There was a big blue sky and green grass on a gently rolling hill with big striped tents like a circus. There was a big group of people and someone was giving instructions for a game with four parts: A, B, C & D. I really needed the bathroom so didn't really pay attention to the instructions but at the same time couldn't pull myself away to go and find the bathroom. I was torn and not concentrating on anything that was being said.

When the games started, I had no idea what was going on and people had to take my piece of paper away to scribble the correct answers on it. I felt like a naughty schoolgirl, not having paid attention nor done my homework. I missed the end of the game as well because I turned my head and the next minute the whole field was completely empty of people!

Am I missing something important in my life? What am I not paying proper attention to? Is it the elephant on the table or something else?

The rest of the day was spent busily reading and taking notes from the recommended reading list. The dream also woke me up to the reality of the situation regarding the training course. There is so much preparation that I need to be doing right now. The face-to-face part of the course is only a couple of days long. The better informed and aware I am when I go into it, the more I will be able to get out of it.

My reading today was about the birth process and how it happens physiologically, including the different hormones involved in each stage. It also mentions what can interfere with the natural process and make it stop. This includes learning the interventions that are available, along with their pros and cons. I enjoyed reading about the history of childbirth through the ages as a way to better understand the present situation.

There were also books to read about how to really listen to someone else, without judgement or giving advice. To assist the speaker to find their own path to the solution that is right for them, which might be different from what you think is right for them. Challenging stuff, especially when you really think you know what is best for someone. But that was what I had intuitively done with Jelly when she needed to talk about her feelings. Maybe it was easier because I didn't know. Sometimes ignorance is easier than knowing too much.

I had time for half an hour at the allotment to finish the winter pruning of the raspberries and currants. This set them up for the coming growing season along with a thick blanket of potash from the wood burner topped with a layer of rotted manure. It may be smelly, dirty work now but I know in a few months it will pay me back with big lush fruit full of juicy flavour. It's a small price to pay. A heavy rain started as I was leaving so the manure mulch will help to retain that wetness in the soil where the plants need it most right now.

Thursday 4th March

I have nearly finished packing my weekend bag for the course which begins tomorrow. I feel nervous. Yesterday's dream still lingers, holding the memory of the confusion of not understanding instructions, nor listening to my body's needs. Why didn't I just listen to my own needs, go to the bathroom and ask someone to help me when I got back? It was like I didn't want to be weak and leave, but by doing that I lost out completely.

My route is printed out, snacks packed for the drive, car checked for oil, water, tyre pressure, full tank of petrol. Jelly is on call to feed the cats. Although I didn't know if it was appropriate asking her so soon after she has given birth. She insisted. 'It'll get me out of the house, and I'll enjoy sitting here with Valentina, looking at the view, giving her a feed and stroking the cats.'

She knows my floppy cats so well. They love being pampered by her and having someone sit with them for a while, not just plunking down their food like the neighbour does. Well, the neighbour is a dear to do it, being allergic to cats and all, so I don't like asking her if I can possibly help it. Jelly's dog loves the cats as well. He comes in wagging his tail at them and before you know it they're rolling around together on the mat like long lost brothers from different mothers.

It has nearly been three weeks since the beginning of Valentina's life and also three weeks since the beginning of my new life. I still can hardly believe I'm doing the training this weekend. How did it all happen so fast?

Yesterday, the suggested reading went well, but there is still so much information I've yet to uncover. The sheer amount of things to learn as well as the different areas and wealth of resources that are available and those still developing, are staggering.

This natural birth movement is relatively new in some ways, reclaiming birth out of the hospitals and away from the bright lights. It believes that women are capable of giving birth without routine medical intervention. But it probably needs to be understood within the larger context of history about how birth moved into hospital in the first place, the history of our beliefs about childbirth. The commonly held belief about the best place for giving birth has changed over the ages. Popular belief has moved from home to hospital and now back to home again for some.

The medical profession had learnt some incredible ways to save lives. Back in the Dark Ages, many women went into childbirth wondering if they would survive the ordeal. But does modern day medicine understand what a birthing mother needs in order for the natural birth hormones to flow? The medicalization of childbirth was welcomed when it began saving countless lives and reducing what was seen as unnecessary pain. But has it over-stepped the line? It's difficult to know when there are so many different opinions on the issue. So many groups doing what they believe is right. Some say there is no need to put yourself through any pain ~ just have a caesarean. Others say the best place to be is at home with people you love around you. Conventional opinions are being challenged not only in the field of childbirth but in so many areas: education, traditional careers, marriage, and health. So many strong opinions mixed with contradictory scientific research, depending on who is doing the research and who is funding it.

I understand the process of birth from what I have read. Labour begins with the gentle building of contractions as the cervix tilts forward and thins in preparation for birth. Contractions then increase in speed and intensity as the muscles of the uterus create waves of muscle contractions that work together to push the baby down the birth canal, the short passage through the pelvis where baby spirals, turning to birth the head, then shoulders, then body.

There is the delicate interplay of hormones that directs the process from backstage. The birth isn't really over until the delivery of the placenta that nourished and sustained the baby through nine intimate months.

Then there is the important first hour after birth, the bonding time when mother and baby see each other face-to-face for the very first time and get to know each other by sight, smell, touch and taste.

Then begins the so-called fourth trimester where the new family readjusts to life, transitions to a new state of being, with new rhythms, routines and sleep cycles. Yet this balance is delicate, easily interrupted and disturbed.

Only by knowing the wide range of normal can it begin to become apparent when something is outside those boundaries and a medical intervention can become a real life-saver instead of an unnecessary manipulation. The road is wide and I have a long path in front of me.

Friday 5th March

Morning: This is it. The weekend begins here. I'm setting off in half an hour. The car is already packed, with music in the CD player and flask at the ready. Here is the opportunity to write about how I feel right now, in this moment, because by this evening things will have changed and nothing will be as it was. Or maybe nothing will change. But I suspect it will.

There are seven other women on the course, with me filling the last available place. A small group to promote trust and bonding, the blurb had said. I wonder who they are, these seven other women. How did their paths lead them to seek training? Where do they come from and why are they doing this? What is it exactly that we are doing? What is a Doula? What does a Doula do, or not do?

Why am I suddenly feeling nervous, sweaty palms and racing heart? I suppose it could be the large coffee I just filled up on! Okay, time is up and I am off.

Later in the afternoon: After meeting these fascinating women, I sat here trying to remember each of their stories:

Leanne is the course's Doula trainer and has been teaching for two years. She used to be a National Childbirth Trust antenatal teacher and was a swimming teacher before that. I guess teaching must be in her blood. She has four children, two born in hospital, two born at home. In her career she has attended over a hundred births as a Doula.

Susan is a housewife and mother to two kids aged four and two. She has had natural births and wants to help other women achieve the same.

Harriet, an older woman (in her sixties), is grandmother to twelve children! She is mother to four adult children, all born at home. She has attended a few births over the years, including many of her grandchildren, and now wants to be more up-to-date with her knowledge.

Beatrice used to be in PR until giving birth to her son, eighteen months ago. That experience totally changed her view of the world and she is now looking at a career change.

Helen is a mother of two adult children. She feels drawn to being with women and now has the time to dedicate herself to the calling.

Claire brought her youngest with her, four month-old Helen. She also has an eight year-old and a six year-old.

Sarah has one daughter.

Clarissa is a mother who lives in a yurt with her two or three kids (I can't remember how many) in a community where there is a need for a birth attendant and antenatal teacher. Many women in her community are getting pregnant. Clarissa felt drawn to be that person and the community has supported her financially to be here.

I first noted as their stories unfolded that they all have children. Is it a requirement? Was there some small print I failed to read? Then the other doubts started.

How could I think this could possibly be my path with no personal experience of giving birth? I haven't been through it. I can't possibly know what women are going through. I sat in the circle feeling smaller and smaller and waiting for an opportunity to make my excuses and disappear.

Finally my turn came to speak, to introduce myself and briefly explain why I was here. What brought me to be sitting in the circle? Actually it was a surprise to hear myself talk, to feel the strength of my feeling as I explained why I feel the calling. The passion that drives me to be a Doula was born along with Valentina. Sharing some of her birth story felt natural. I'm not a natural speaker and speaking in front of a group of eight people made me nervous at first. But it flowed out.

Watching their reactions to how Valentina slid into my hands was interesting. It dawned on me even more the magnitude of what happened that day.

None of them had been at a birth like that and they said that they were in awe of such an experience. Some of the others had told sad or traumatic birth stories which contrasted with Valentina's.

During the tea break I approached Leanne and asked her opinion about being a Doula without being a mother as well. She explained that although most Doulas are mothers, it is certainly not a requirement. There are a few exceptional Doulas who have never given birth and yet excel in the profession. Not having children at home gives the freedom of not having to arrange childcare or balance work and family commitments. Being on call can be stressful and having childcare ready twenty four hours a day for the period when your client is due to give birth is not always easy. Her children are all teenagers now, old enough to cope for themselves during her absences. But I wondered about the other women on the course. I was curious about the ones still breastfeeding or with toddlers at home. How will they manage?

Leanne also mentioned that giving birth could be an empowering experience but it could also be a hard experience. If there had been any unresolved issues from their own births, a Doula might bring that personal baggage with them while attending a birth, thereby affecting the birthing room. It was something for me to think about but there was so much other information to take in that it got pushed to the back of my mind as we resumed the class.

So what does a Doula actually *do*? The question was addressed today and my pen raced over the lines in the notebook in an attempt to keep up with the ever expanding list.

~ A mother for the mother
~ Birth attendant
~ Listener
~ Emotional support
~ Makes tea
~ Supports the father in supporting the mother
~ Supports whole family, including siblings
~ A calm presence
~ Knows hospital procedures, pros & cons
~ Knowledge of the various interventions available
~ Holds belief in the mother
~ Knows the mother and supports her birth plan
~ Non-judgemental with whatever may come up

~ Confidential
~ Trustworthy
~ Physically strong
~ Mentally strong
~ Has knowledge of birth physiology and anatomy
~ Knows what normal birth is like
~ Spots deviations from the norm
~ Sees warning signs
~ Helps with care of new-born
~ Breastfeeding support
~ Helps with running the home in the early days
~ Can do light housework so mother can concentrate on the new-born
~ Also runs own business, finding clients and marketing

Saturday 6th March

Language is powerful. That fact really came home this morning during the group session. We were looking at how the power of communication is central to a Doula's role.

Most of us had cried during an exercise to debrief our own births, not of our children but the moment we ourselves came into the world from our mother's wombs. Until then I had never realized how deeply I felt about the huge gap I have in the story of my life. My birth has never been mentioned, no stories were ever told about the day I arrived. I have no idea how I was born. I never felt able to ask and was never told. Hardly even seeing my mother these days, I prefer to keep the distance as an emotional safety barrier between us. Her words are wielded like knives, sharp knives.

My father is a mysterious figure shrouded in misleading stories and dead ends. The stories would change every time his name came up, which wasn't often. I have often thought that this 'not telling' of where he went and what really happened is another barrier that keeps mother and me apart.

So I didn't have much to share during that exercise. I cried, of course. It felt like such a safe space in which to let down the mask of appearing to cope with not knowing who I am. The tears were also for the emotional distance I feel from the woman who gave me life. I have no idea who she really is, if truth be known.

Truth and honesty are so intrinsic to love that in their absence, doubt and suspicion grow. After today, however, the desire to wrestle with the ghosts of the past has returned to me. To really talk with my mother and find out what happened. Never in my life had it even crossed my mind to look for my father. My partner in today's exercise asked me if I had looked for him, to hear his side to the story, and I just stared at her as if she was speaking a foreign language.

I know his name as it appears on my birth certificate: Harold Benjamin Thorpe. It's a small miracle in itself that the certificate survived this long, being ripped to pieces during mother's rages and taped back together to be returned to the drawer. Until one day when I slipped it into my suitcase as I walked out to start another life, a life where unanswered questions didn't stare me down every morning over my bowl of cereal. Where I could be free to forget and get on with living in the moment.

I had chosen to paint the crashing of the waves and the soaring of the seagulls in a town far away from the lies and contradictory information. My brother still goes back, says he feels it's his duty to be there for her, to repent all that has gone before. Was that when we were young and he sat there and listened to her rip my self-esteem to shreds. I can't say I understand his pious calling. Shouldn't I be the one he is consoling? It shows how we both went in completely opposite directions. I wanted to get as far away as possible from it, he virtually moved in next door.

Maybe my father is still alive. Maybe he's not dead at all. Maybe he has an email or is on Facebook. Maybe I could find him if I were to look. Do I want to? There are a lot of maybes involved in those questions. Today I have had enough searching, and cried enough tears over the past.

I arrived back at my rented room this evening as if it were a different country, feeling like I have travelled a long way. I have learnt new ways of looking at things which challenge my preconceived notions of the world and my place in it.

Looking again at the birthing room, dynamics between midwives, doctors, health care staff, Doulas and parents-to-be are intricate and complex. Everyone trying to do what they believe is best or have been trained to believe is the best. How does a Doula navigate her way through all that without trying to control the steering of the whole ship in the direction that she wishes it to go? How does she fully support the parents in their decisions? Oh, this could be the 'Art of Doula-ing' or maybe 'To Do The Doula.' We are

English, let us verb our nouns and noun our verbs. Grammatical rules are strangely flexible and law-defying.

Sunday 7th March

On the way home tonight, after the course had finished and the last hug had been given with promises to stay in touch, a roadside café called me to sit within its warm walls and sip some tea. Sitting here I am surrounded by plastic plants and dazed looking drivers wandering in from their journeys as much in need of coffee as they are fuel for their cars. I don't feel as dazed as they look but I certainly do not feel like I did when I drove past this café on Friday. I feel so different in such a short space of time. In a way, I feel my whole existence has been challenged, if challenged is the right word. Questioned may be a better one.

How did I come into this world? Why was I never really told why my father left? Why did I never ask? Why do I feel such emptiness when I imagine what it was like for me as a baby? Why do the memories hurt? So many questions bubbling up that I couldn't drive any longer; I needed to stop and write them down to get them out of my head and ease the internal pressure.

I realize how archaic I must look, crouched over the table with my pot of tea, my pen making these squiggly lines on paper. Here I am, scribbling these letters and words, when all around me the tables are full of people tapping into the sleek black icon of modern civilization with its instant worldwide connection.

There is a family two tables over having a Skype conversation on their iPhone with people in Japan. I can't understand what they're saying but I'm guessing they're talking about the weather and the fact that they're talking from a roadside café full of potted plastic plants and English people drinking tea, and that there is one woman who is actually still writing something with a pen and paper.

After this weekend, the realization is forming that I do not become a Doula merely by having a certificate or by attending a couple of births. To be a Doula is something more akin to a life path, a journey that is walked day by day and the learning continues throughout life, growing and encompassing a wide range of experiences and knowledge. Every book read, every birth attended, every new baby greeted, every new family born, every training course and teleconference participated in, every woman met, every story shared becomes a part of a living reality. These experiences are my teachers now. Life itself has become my master and I am the humble student. As long as there is life, there will be learning. There are always new avenues to explore and new ideas to be hatched. I am excited about this, the idea of this training being a springboard for the future, in more ways than one. After completing this course, I am able register with a national organization and after completing their requirements, I can advertise as a fully qualified Doula.

Before we finished earlier today, we learnt more about the anatomy and physiology of birth. I loved it. In my head I was in my studio sketching pregnant women ~ the way they hold themselves, the curve of the belly and arch of the back, the stance of the feet and holding of the shoulders. Today I learnt a more fully informed respect for the amazing flexibility of the pelvis and the journey the baby takes through a space perfectly fitted to its shape and dimension. What a miracle of human engineering the pelvis is. The joints can actually stretch in between the bones in preparation for birth. The baby turns and spirals out to be able to fit through the space exactly.

We watched videos of women in natural labour this afternoon to become more aware of what was normal in order to recognize when something moved over into the realm of abnormal. We saw how these women moved around into different positions, thereby jiggling the baby around into the optimum position for the descent out of the watery world into this world of air and earth.

We also talked about the human mammal and our hormonal and physiological similarities with other mammals. I remembered the dream I had a while ago about the whales. Our mammalian brains with their neo-cortex are an evolution from the primal brain of other animals. This new addition to our cerebral cortex regulates our endocrine system, which controls the oxytocin and adrenalin flow, among other things. All mammals seek a similar environment to give birth ~ somewhere quiet and safe. We need to feel safe for the right hormones to flow and we need the right hormones to flow to give birth. The introduction of artificial hormones into the bloodstream can inhibit the flow of the body's natural secretions.

My training has really begun and I am on the road, but not alone. I feel like I am walking in the footsteps of all the wise women who have gone before me and forged the path. I have their support and am feeling safe as I set out on this journey. I also have Leanne as a mentor. For the first two births I attend as a trainee Doula, I will debrief with her afterwards over the phone about how the birth went. This way she will be available to help with any questions that I have.

I still have a lot of reading to do and a couple of assignments to complete, as well as attending two births with my mentor before I finish this course. It all feels within the realms of possibility, if I can believe in myself and carry on with this new workload. This weekend brought up a lot of personal things for me, which I was not expecting to be part of our training.

Digging into my own past, into the relationship with my parents and the events of my own birth, was emotional. I have not connected with those memories for a long time. They bring up too many unanswered questions, too much pain, and it is all too much for me to contain sometimes.

I am not alone in the emotional baggage I carry under my day-to-day appearance. The other women who are also sharing this journey with me had their own pasts to confront this weekend. Does everyone carry things until the right moment presents itself to be able to let go?

Leanne had shared with us that this was one of the biggest parts of the training. How could we be able to support others during such an emotional and vulnerable time as childbirth if we had not heard and healed our own hurts?

We heard how many people who are drawn to work with birth do so because on an unconscious level they are crying out to heal their own. Dealing with this now and not having to play out our own personal dramas at someone else's expense can make for a much cleaner birthing environment for the people we work with.

It does, however, make it messy for us here in the present, having to work through our own hurts and letting go of those unconscious patterns. How much have the events surrounding my own birth and early childhood affected me? Do I unconsciously attract situations to myself to play out these patterns over and over again? There are so many questions, so much to process.

The tea has gone cold and my bed is calling. It is time to pack up my old pens and paper and go home.

Monday 8th March

Today I had much time to sit and think after I heard that Anne-Marie was unable to receive me today. I found this out when her housemaid called to apologise. She hoped this wouldn't inconvenience me and would expect me tomorrow at the same time if that was agreeable to me. It was, and so with time on my hands today, I sat.

I sat in the big chair looking out of the window, then sat on the beach watching the waves break, and later sat on a bench at the harbour watching the gulls grabbing pieces of fish. I sat in the park looking at spring bulbs, sat at the table looking at the food on my plate, sat in the studio looking at a piece waiting for attention, sat and looked at the onion sets waiting to be planted, sat on the sofa looking at the fire, and sat in bed looking at the wall.

It's like my brain was mixing a cake, going around and around, all the different ingredients all thrown in. Valentina and the midwives and Leanne and the Doula course and the stories of each of the seven women and

Anne-Marie and my mother and father, and the different feelings I have about my own birth and about attending someone else's. Quite a concoction!

I am more than happy to support someone during her birth, to put flannels on her forehead, to give drinks, to massage her back, to hear her story, to do what needs to be done. But to think about how my own birth might have been? The thought strikes me like an icy trickle down my back. To imagine being looked after as a helpless infant by my mother is an almost impossible task. She can hardly look after herself. She is so self-absorbed that I'm honestly surprised I survived the ordeal with only anger and detachment to show for it. Yet deep down inside I know I have to make peace with these intense emotions associated with how I came into the world.

Birth workers can bring trauma with them, Leanne had said. At first I was surprised at this. Surely most birth workers have taken up this work to help, support and encourage the best possible outcome for their clients. What is this about bringing trauma with them? It just feels like such a negative starting place. Sometimes I don't feel so traumatized. Besides, I have managed to live my entire life thus far without hearing my birth story. Do I really need to know it now?

Tuesday 9th March

I met with Anne-Marie for the second time this morning, at her house. There were more fabulous French pastries and coffee overlooking the gardens. I felt somewhat more qualified now that I have started my official training.

Anne-Marie continued to gush on about how wonderful it was that she had found me and how grateful she was. I asked if she had been unwell yesterday but she just shook her head and evaded the question. I didn't push any more. It was obvious that whatever had happened, she didn't want to talk about it.

In the days since our last meeting she had been reading up on statistics, which show that having a Doula at the birth reduces the need for interventions and often means less pain relief. I didn't mention my personal concerns about past birth trauma (mine nor hers). It had been mentioned during our training that it could be beneficial to talk about these things with an expectant mother before her birth. But today it somehow seemed inappropriate to talk about it when Anne-Marie was so happy and excited.

The question I did ask was if she had any fears about the coming birth. She replied, 'Not having it all go to plan and losing control is my biggest fear.'

Yes, she likes to be in charge ~ the queen of her castle and mistress of her domain.

Again I stayed for hours and eventually left exhausted. I am still not entirely clear on what is expected of me during the birth itself, but her optimism is infectious. The expected due date is Saturday so already I am on call as a Doula for my first birth.

At home I packed a bag to put by the door, ready for when that call comes. I was sure to add a good handbook for being a birth assistant, full of ideas, tips, and practical advice. I also packed my own bag with all the things I might need for spending a night away from home, as well as some extra comfort items like essential oils and massage oil. I put in speakers and my iPod with

Anne-Marie's play list already copied onto it. My phone and charger are also ready to jump into the bag. I felt excited packing and wondered how long it would be until I used the bag.

Wednesday 10th March

The weather is deliciously warm today. It feels like the first whiff of summer is around the corner. Digging at the allotment and feeling the warm sun was like heaven. Sitting outside the shed drinking from my flask of tea, I closed my eyes and could have been on a foreign shore for the power of my imagination.

Sally, the midwife I met at Jelly's birth, came by and I showed her around, sharing my plans and ideas for the coming season. In addition to her knowledge of birthing, she obviously knows a thing or two about gardening. We shared some sandwiches and I updated her on my Doula journey. Being on call for a birth is something that she has gotten used to. The waiting for the phone to ring, then the two o'clock-in-the-morning calls and late nights all go with the territory of being a midwife.

Thursday 11th March

I dreamt of a big shire horse with long white feathers around his feet last night. I was helping to get him ready for a long journey somewhere. His keeper was a sprite elf and the horse was enchanted by a thin rope around his neck. The thin rope, however, took away his powerful strength so the sprite elf decided to replace it with a normal-sized rope. This allowed the horse to have his own strength and will, to be able to pull his heavy load. The question was what would he do once free of the enchanted rope ~ continue to work or break free? I do not know what happened next because at that moment one of the cats jumped up on the bed, landing on my head. But the image of this giant beast kept docile with a tiny thread has stuck with me. It reminds me of elephant training. Baby elephants are bound with chains they cannot break. But when they grow big and strong enough to break these chains they don't because they have been conditioned to believe they cannot. Such is the power of belief.

I wondered about my beliefs. Were there things about the world that I believed to be true simply because I had accepted them as fact? These past few weeks have been forcing me to reassess my life, my priorities, my strengths and weaknesses. It is as though I am waking up out of an enchanted sleep and beginning to look around me with fresh eyes. I see things I never noticed before. Perhaps the time is coming closer for me to throw off my enchanted rope and be free from the shackles of the past.

Coming back to the present, Hilary told me stories about her youth today. We drank tea from china cups at a polished oak table with a view over the park. Slices of fresh home-baked carrot cake with lemon icing sat on a silver tray before us.

I loved listening to her stories. They were almost like tales from another country. She had not told me exactly how old she was, though I had guessed seventy or seventy five. When she told me she was ninety four, I nearly dropped my china teacup. Daily walks, sea swimming, a wholesome diet as well as an optimistic outlook on life were her prescription for longevity. I was very impressed.

The conversation moved to birth and Hilary shared how, back in her youth, home birth was the norm. She gave birth to four sons in her own bed. They were big strapping lads who were born without any problems, except for one of them. Her youngest son was born a couple of weeks early, her regular midwife was on holiday and wasn't able to attend the birth. Instead she had this burly brute of a woman who slapped her legs and told her, 'Just git on wiv it and stop complaining will ya, yu got yerself in this mess in the first place.'

More from fear of being slapped again than any bodily desire, Hilary pushed for all she was worth. She ejected her huge fourth child so quickly into the world that her perineum tore severely. That injury itself took hours to sew up and weeks to heal completely. Luckily the brute's shift ended soon after the actual birth and another midwife came to stitch her up. This one cooed and ahhed over the baby, trying to ease some of the pain and shock Hilary was feeling after the violent birth.

That was her fourth and final child. The tear was so severe, the doctor warned, that another birth might cause the scar to rupture and she was advised against any more pregnancies.

Looking at Hilary, it was hard to imagine anyone slapping her for any reason. But telling that story brought tears to her eyes and mine. She told of the difficulty she had bonding with the child that had split her so severely. To this day she sees herself treating him differently from his brothers, although almost imperceptibly. The scars of his birth ran deeper than the stitches. The boys are all grown men now, most with children of their own.

Hilary attended three of her grandchildren's births when her daughter-in-law asked her to be present. The woman's own mother had died when she was young and she felt Hilary was a second mother to her. The love was mutual. Hilary was delighted to have the daughter she'd never had.

But those birth stories would have to wait for another time. We left her flat and descended the huge winding staircase through the shared hall to walk the dogs before dusk. I said goodbye and walked quietly home, enjoying the feeling of having made a new friend, someone with a lot of life experience, such a wealth of wisdom and knowledge.

Friday 12th March

Today I was digging out my old foes ~ the perennial weeds. It's all about addressing the balance between respecting nature and exerting my will over the primal forces. A constant realigning is necessary if I wish to cultivate the patch of land staked and named as my allotment.

As I dig up beds for the new season, I allow some time for the weeds to show themselves and be removed before I sow. Some seeds are already in the ground, protected from the elements by the cloches.

The rain came while I was digging, so I sat in the shed watching it pour down and preparing my seaweed potion. Feeling like an old witch, I stirred the concoction of seaweed before straining it for spraying over the seedlings. The old guys on the other allotments swear that this seaweed concoction is the stuff that wins their vegetables prizes in the country shows. That and other tricks they've got up their sleeves, no doubt. Tricks they won't go around telling people about.

My grandpa used to spend every day on his allotment, growing the most amazing vegetables. He whispered his secret into my ear one day when I was about seven years old. I used to spend all my spare time with him in those years. He used to call me his little apprentice.

I remember how he leant down close to my ear to whisper this secret. His leathery brown hand, covered in a fine layer of rich dark soil, held up to his mouth so no one else would hear these words destined only for me. The smell of tobacco filled my nose, making it crinkle a little to tease him as he whispered.

'You gotta talk to 'em, see. Gotta tell 'em you love 'em and how happy you'll be when they grow big and strong.'

'Talk to 'em?' I turned to him incredulously, 'You what?'

'Yes, my little 'prentice. Talking to the plants is the best way of getting them to grow for you. If you don't love 'em and don't tell 'em, they won't grow well. Took me years to learn that,' he whispered.

'It was my own great-grandfather who told me that when I was but a boy. I, too, thought he was a bit soft in the head until I tried it. Never looked back when I did, and neither should you. Trust in the olden ways,' he confided, with a wink of his old brown eye.

I squinted at him, this gentle giant of a man who had taken me under his wing and had given me an escape from home, from mother.

I had my own corner of his huge allotment from when I was five. Growing mainly weeds and digging holes, I think, in those days. But he never said anything, just told me how to care for the tools and treat them with respect. When I was a bit older, I started pushing seeds into the dark earth and marvelling when seedlings appeared, to later grow into big plants and give food.

Pumpkins were my favourite thing to grow. They were big, happy-looking orange things and I loved them. Mother hated them for some inexplicable reason so grandpa took them home, cooked up soups and stews and we shared them together secretly.

Days like today I remember my old grandpa, sitting in his shed on his allotment, tools gleaming and plants blooming around him in the soil dug and cared for by his hands for so many years. Life teased from its dark and loamy depths.

Even though he's been gone for years I still feel him here with me. I hear his voice in my head when I am wondering what to do about a problem or how to manage a certain plant that won't grow so well. His cap still hangs on a nail on the back of the door in my shed. I took it with me when I left. No one knows it's there. Mother was clinical in her clearing out of all his things from every corner of our lives when he passed away, like she wanted to forget he even existed. I hid some things up on his allotment, buried them in the ground to prevent anyone finding them.

I dug them out before the allotment was passed onto new hands. Silly really as they were only little things. There was a small cup for first prize we had won at a county fayre. He had entered my vegetables under his name since I was too young to enter them myself. It was our secret. Mother would never have allowed me to enter. I also hid the silver framed photo of his wedding day to my grandma, who passed away while giving birth to my mother. Finally, there was my grandma's wedding ring, which he placed in my hand the last time I saw him alive.

'You keep this safe, young 'un,' he had told me. 'There'll come a day when a young man will be wanting to make a respectable woman of you and this'll be yours to wear that day. Your grandma would've liked that.'

At the time, I didn't know why he was giving it to me. Maybe he knew he was ill and felt that the end was nearer than any of us imagined. Maybe he just wanted to give it to me before it was too late.

That weekend had been his last. They found him at the allotment, cold and still. Heart attack, they'd said. I think it was a broken heart. He had known I was only staying around for him. There was nowhere else in that town where I could have escaped my mother. So he'd left first, leaving me free to do what I wanted with the rest of my life.

I stayed for the funeral, silently crying the tears I was unable to shed. A couple of weeks later, I'd dug the things up from the ground and left town for good.

I don't often remember those times. Today reminded me so much of the days we would spend together on the allotment, working, talking, laughing, eating and living side by side. They were happy days.

Today was a happy day. A quiet kind of sad-happy day remembering grandpa and the times we spent together. I still miss him even after all these years.

Saturday 13th March

Tomorrow will mark Valentina's first month of life, a life already blessed in many ways. Jelly and Nick have decided to have a celebration. They'd been wrapped up in their own safe space these past four weeks and felt it was time to share their happiness with their circle of friends and extended family.

Of course I offered to help prepare the food. I love to cook. I spent this morning shopping and organizing.

This afternoon Jelly had cabin fever so we took a break from preparing food to have a walk. The warm sun felt good as we strolled along the beach and through the park. The park was blazing with colour after winter and the bright sun seemed to highlight the striking colours of spring flowers. Blossoms were dripping from the trees, adding to the feeling that we were walking in a wonderland.

A couple of familiar dogs came rushing around a corner, followed closely by Hilary. She was delighted to meet Jelly and baby Valentina after I had shared so much about them with her. I listened to the two of them chatting away like old friends, heard the birds singing from the nearby trees, and felt the sun on my face. A smile crept over my face as I watched Valentina sleeping snugly amid this explosion of spring life. It all amounted to a deep happiness at simple pleasures.

Sunday 14th March

A day celebrated with family and friends. The morning started off with the four of us having breakfast together. We were noticing all the little things Valentina does now that she wasn't doing a month ago.

How her legs have straightened out, showing she's been getting used to all the space she now has to stretch out after the confines of the womb. She is awake for longer periods of time and seems able to see more now as she fixes people with her gaze and enjoys looking at windows and shadows. It's amazing when you hold her and she looks deep into your face, intently staring and copying your facial expressions, poking out her little tongue or opening eyes wide in surprise.

Her happiest sounds come just before feeding, which after those difficult first days, has become something easy and natural for both of them. Nick realizes how much he can support Jelly in breastfeeding by bringing pillows, drinks and food when she sits down to feed the baby. The little things he does to show Jelly just how much he cares about her and supports her breastfeeding have helped to push away those dark clouds. Valentina has this blissful drunken stupor when she drops off the breast at the end of a feed, eyelids fluttering, mouth open, and drool hanging out.

Loads of people turned up to toast the baby. It was the first public gathering and a wonderful show of love. All the women who were at the baby shower before the birth were there. Although they had been always been supportive in their thoughts, this had been the first time they had all been together since before the birth. Birthing stories were shared. We went over and over Valentina's birth story ~ how she had slipped into my surprised hands before the midwife had been called and gazed open-eyed at these two women looking down at her.

There was an appreciation of photos from the last month, an ode to Valentina. I am sure that Nick will have a few more photography contracts coming through after that amazing display of his skill with the camera.

Monday 15th March

I went back to my other work today, which involves dealing with the gallery owner, negotiating, talking, and bargaining.

Communication has always been a huge part of the negotiating. Did he hear what I was trying to tell him? Could I hear what he was saying?

I used some of the techniques from the Doula course and it was great. Echoing back what I thought I'd heard for clarification meant what was said and what was heard were the same things. Also using the correct body language to show I was interested and listening made me realize that often our past conversations had been done to each other's backs as we'd wandered around the gallery. We had mixed chatting with business and we had both come away confused about what had been decided. Good listening skills = good outcome. Today was testimony to that.

Tonight I had supper at Marilyn's house. We briefly talked about Anne-Marie, as it was Marilyn that brought us together. But the conversation quickly turned to art as it normally does whenever we get together. It was wonderful to share the excitement for my new stone balancing compositions. I also enjoyed catching up with her current work focus, which is full of bright colours. I felt like I had stepped into Mardi Gras, it was so vibrant and alive.

Tuesday 16th March

This morning included an hour of at my allotment. The last of the winter brassica came out and the bed was made ready for something new. I'm still holding off planting my seedlings. Although the days are getting warmer, the clear skies at night have been giving way to frost in the morning. The greenhouse is filling up with more seed trays and life is relentlessly pushing up through the earth, as there is no holding it back.

This afternoon was not so quiet. It was spent with Anne-Marie and her ever-increasing bump. Her due date is approaching and she is keen to give birth. The heaviness of the baby and the tiredness she is feeling combine to make her wish it were over. She certainly wasn't as sprightly today as previous visits. She moved slowly and with care.

While massaging her back as she leant forward over a pile of cushions I felt her relax under my hands. Later we talked over her birth plan. As I listened I realized I had not yet met her husband, Larry, and thought how strange it would be not to meet him until the birthing time.

Anne-Marie brushed off my concerns, 'It will all work out fine. He will be there.' She made it sound as if being there was sufficient. 'Larry is very busy right now, tying up all the loose ends before the baby arrives,' she explained as we were looking at the framed photos that lined the hall.

I looked at recent photos of a dark haired man in a tux with his arms around her; she was dressed in the largest white meringue explosion of a wedding dress. It was a miracle alone that he could get his arms around her. She looked divinely happy, gazing into his eyes devotedly. He stared at the camera, or close to it, with a look of triumph or pride in his eyes.

There were also photos of the dogs: in the river, in the fields, on the beach, in the heather. How would the dogs feel about having a baby in the house? I wondered silently to myself.

As I left Anne-Marie tapped me on the arm. 'Keep your phone on, it won't be long now,' she whispered to me conspiratorially. How did she know?

But I couldn't ask her as she turned on her heel and swept back into the house, the dogs at her heels. The lady of the manor.

Wednesday 17th March

After yesterday's meeting, I revised my preparations for the coming birth. I filled the car with petrol, found a purse with small change for the parking meter, and checked my Doula bag again. It feels like only a couple of days ago I was doing this for the Doula course. The birth could be any day now. I dare not go too far away from town on trips. I keep my mobile phone on me at all times, checking it often for missed calls. But it remains quiet. I remembered Sally's stories about being on call.

I found Hilary on the beach with the dogs. We walked together and discussed the weather and simple things. She invited me in for a pot of tea, which was very welcome. We talked about waiting ~ waiting for the tea to brew, the sea to go out, the sun to set, the summer to come, and the baby to be born. Hilary inspires me with her calm, patient ways. Her bright blue eyes shine from beneath her white hair. She has seen so much of life, experienced so many things through her years. Maybe one day I will have lived long enough to have the sense of perspective that she has learned and will inherit her sense of deep calm in the world.

Thursday 18th March

We are still waiting. It is the projected due date tomorrow based on medical calculations. Nature may have different plans. I spoke with Anne-Marie on the phone today. The only change in her condition is that she has heartburn. She is seeing the midwife tomorrow for a membrane sweep.

Friday 19th March

The D-day has come and almost gone. It is eleven o'clock in the evening now so no baby is coming today.

Anne-Marie was in tears on the phone earlier. She really wanted to give birth today. The good news is that the heartburn has gone. The baby has engaged by dropping into the pelvis which is a sign it is getting ready to be born and makes a bit more space for mother's organs. Anne-Marie has been busy scrubbing and cleaning, cooking and baking, trying to keep busy and moving. I urged her to rest as well but don't know if she heard me. Perhaps I also need to rest to prepare for whatever lies ahead.

Saturday 20th March

What a wild day today. The wind was battling the trees and whipping them around. The sea was raging, covered in white horses galloping into the shore to smash on the rocks. Lashing rain was drenching everything. Visibility was blurred with thick clouds hanging low, hugging the lay of the land. Boats buck and rear as they pull against their moorings with a seemingly conscious intent to break loose and join the white horses so free on the open waves. Cars slink slowly by, their wipers vainly attempting to hold back the torrents of water falling from the sky. Not an optimal day for going into labour.

The phone rang at ten o'clock, just as I wa getting ready for bed, and my heart jumped when I heard Anne-Marie's voice on the other end. There was no alarm, just to tell me she was feeling something was happening and wanted to share it with me. Larry was home with her. She wasn't alone and felt fine, though perhaps a little nervous, I thought.

Sunday 21st March

Another phone call came at two o'clock this morning. Her contractions had started. They were coming and going with no regular pattern yet. She said they weren't very strong and that she was coping with them. Larry could be heard in the background talking. I wondered to whom at that time of night, most likely the midwife. I asked if I should go over to their house but in the end we decided I could wait and come over later.

At six she phoned again to let me know that a mucus show had just come. I noticed that the sound of her voice had changed. She sounded nervous and not quite so sure about things now the labour was actually happening. I knew it was time for me to go over. She didn't have to ask. I could tell by the slight panic edging her words. Luckily, the weather calmed and roads are clear.

9am. Anne-Marie's contractions don't seem to be increasing; she is not pleased. It feels like she is trying to use her will alone to get them to speed up but they aren't listening.

She paces the room jiggling her belly, 'Hurry up, come on.'

I've been sitting quietly in the corner of their opulent bedroom for a couple of hours as she paces and pants. Larry is using the app on his phone to time the contractions and is totally absorbed with it. That is, when he isn't using the phone to talk to his associates, which he seems to be doing quite a lot. I've been overhearing talk about golf resorts on the south coast of Spain. Which doesn't seem so appropriate right now but who am I to judge?

Every now and then he leans over and pats her on the behind and says, 'That's my girl.'

She looks at him like a dog that's been given a bone and I have to turn my head away. It feels condescending and makes me feel uncomfortable to watch.

Everyone seems so busy, impatient to get on with the business at hand. Only the baby seems to be hesitant to make an appearance.

Midday. I had to leave. I made an excuse that I needed some air outside. Nobody seemed to notice anyway. It's all feeling very funny. There are strange, stressful dynamics happening and I don't know exactly what is going on. It feels like there is static electricity in the air inside their house. I have to admit, if only to myself, that Larry is driving me crazy with his phone and apparent disinterest of what is happening in the room.

She looks at him hungrily but he only seems to have eyes for his phone.

I tried to gently say something to him.

'Look Larry, I think Anne-Marie would really like some physical support from you right now. I'll take over timing the contractions for a bit.'

In reply, he snapped, 'That's what you're here for.'

I was shocked and didn't know how to respond. Anne-Marie hadn't heard; only the dog looked at me. I thought my role was as second support after him, not in place of him. Images of my role to 'enhance the birth experience' seemed to swim in front of my eyes. What was I really doing there?

I remembered the birth plan and how it was clearly written that Larry was to be present at all times. But now I saw that we never actually discussed what it was he was supposed to be doing. He is on his phone, but he is in the room. He seems to feel that his mere presence is enough. Oh Lord of the manor.

It is time to go back in there now, though it is so peaceful out here. They will be transferring to the birthing unit soon. It is nearly birthing time, I hope.

Midnight. Things are not going well. The transfer to hospital happened really quickly. Before I knew what was happening I was packed off in an ambulance with Anne-Marie. She was refusing to sit up and complaining loudly about the contractions. We had to call an ambulance to come and get her as it didn't seem possible to take her anywhere in the car. We had not discussed who would go with her. I'd assumed Larry would want to, but it wasn't so. He insisted on driving. He had packed all their hospital gear and the baby seat for the journey home.

My car stayed in Little Hengelwook. I did remember to grab my Doula bag from inside before the swirling lights whisked us away. It has felt like being inside a huge whirlwind from the moment I stepped into that vehicle until quite recently. I felt overwhelmed dealing with all the protocol and hospital procedure. The midwives and medical professionals were each offering their two-pence worth on the situation when we arrived. There is no baby yet, and we continue to wait.

Monday 22nd March

10 am. It's quiet here now. Anne-Marie is finally asleep. I'm not sure where Larry is. He left after the epidural went in. The lights have been dimmed and it's peaceful enough in this hospital room. But I'm not in the mood for sleeping, not yet. I have to process what has happened since I stepped into Anne-Marie and Larry's lives, what is still happening, how I am and how Anne-Marie is through all that has happened in the last twenty four hours.

It may be peaceful now but it wasn't earlier. It was crazy. I don't think I have ever seen such a range of raw human emotion in one day. When the pain consumed her she was wide-eyed, screaming as she completely lost control and started clawing at everyone and everything. I was so scared for her. She thought the pain was going to rip her insides out. Everyone was trying to reassure her, but she couldn't or wouldn't hear.

When the anaesthesiologist came to put the epidural in, I was asked to leave. But I could still hear them shouting at each other from where I stood outside the room.

'Mrs Johnston, you have to lie still while I do this or there could be serious repercussions that I do not want to be held responsible for,' the deep voice boomed. It was followed by a familiar voice crying out.

'I am bloody well trying Mr Whatsyourname but there is a arrrggggghhhh it's coming again aarrrggg hhhhhh help me...'

This was followed by a period of deep moaning and the sound of material ripping, which apparently was the blind on the window as Anne-Marie pulled on it too hard.

A woman dressed in hospital gear came along and tapped me on the shoulder as I stood there with my head resting on the wall, arms folded over my chest, eyes closed, listening to the screaming going on.

This woman tapped me on the arm and said something I didn't understand at first. 'She'll get over it,' she had said. She had a little chuckle and walked off. I stared after her retreating back as she went down the corridor, swiped her card at a doorway and pushed through the swinging door to disappear from view. What was that about? Was it meant to reassure me?

We hadn't even made it to the midwifery-led unit when we'd transferred from their home earlier. The ambulance crew took us directly to the hospital. I tried to tell them we were supposed to be going to the birthing unit. They just looked meaningfully at Anne-Marie, who was screaming, and said, 'Not anymore, you're not.'

Something had happened that I wasn't aware of that meant we hadn't been able to go to the midwifery-led unit. I had felt stupid and didn't understand but wasn't able to ask what they meant. The decision had already been made. The hospital had been told to expect us and they were waiting for us when we arrived.

'What am I doing here?' she whimpers to me, as we hold hands waiting for the midwife to come back. I feel stuck for the right words to say.

'You're birthing your baby,' I say. But she shakes her head and looks down.

'My baby doesn't want to be born,' she mumbles.

I take her head in my hands and look into her eyes. 'Your baby is coming, and you are going to be a wonderful mother,' I say, with as much conviction as I can.

She shakes her head free and mumbles something else. But I don't hear it, and before I can ask her to repeat it the midwife appears. We don't have a chance to talk alone again. The midwife does an internal examination and I watch the look of discomfort on Anne-Marie's face.

Larry still hasn't arrived at the hospital. I vaguely wonder if he is having trouble parking his big car in the busy hospital car park.

The midwife withdraws her hand and pulls off the glove with a shake of her head. 'Sorry dear, you're only two centimetres dilated. There's still ever such a long way to go.'

I know her cervix needs to get to ten centimetres dilation. The standard time scale states that a cervix in active labour dilates at one centimetre an hour. Based on these calculations we are looking at eight more hours of labour before the baby descends into the birth canal. But these are only rough calculations, not every birth follows them. Babies can't tell the time.

Anne-Marie crumples at hearing the midwife's words. This is the exact moment that Larry choses to sweep into the room with armfuls of bags, which he drops, to scoop up Anne-Marie and her feelings of inadequacy.

It is a stirring image. I can see the midwife is quite taken with the way this man swoops in like a knight in shining armour. Part of me wonders if perhaps Anne-Marie needs empowering rather than rescuing at this moment.

The tears drip down her face. While patting her back, Larry is questioning the midwife about what they should do now. They are discussing her medication options as if she isn't in the room.

Anne-Marie's head shoots up with a spark of defiance.

'I can do this,' a hidden lioness in her surfaces and roars. I smile as the colour comes back to her cheeks. But it is short-lived.

Larry pats her back and says, 'Yes, dear.' He gives the midwife a look that is both patronising and sympathetic, as if they are to humour his poor deluded wife that she could possibly do it. I feel sick.

The next thing they decide to do is to break her waters. The midwife uses a little stick, saying, 'This might get things going again. You're nice and stretchy down there.'

An hour later nothing has really changed except the stream of doctors and midwives coming and going. A shift change, notes are filled in, questions are asked, tests are done and people are chatting in the corridor. Larry is on his phone.

I felt like a spare part, not knowing what to do. At one point I ask about putting some music on but there is only the radio which talks rubbish and plays trashy songs. I left my iPod and speakers in the car, and in the rush of transfer they had been forgotten.

I try massaging and encouraging her. But she just keeps crying. Larry asks me to leave them alone for a bit.

Now it is the early hours of the morning and we are all exhausted. I don't know what he said to her but when I come back into the room, there has been a change. Anne-Marie is meekly sitting in bed, nodding at a midwife who is explaining about putting a drip of 'jungle juice' into her arm to speed up the contractions. The midwife is saying that Anne-Marie has given natural labour a good go and it hasn't gone to plan so now it is time to use the technology available. This also means having a belt monitor strapped onto her belly as well as the IV drip in her arm.

Anne-Marie looks at Larry who nods ever so slightly. She turns back to the midwife and says something and I can't be sure if I hear it right.

I think she says, 'I'll do whatever is best to get his baby out.' But maybe she really says, 'I'll do whatever is best to get this baby out.' Either way Larry smiles at her in triumph. Whatever he had said to her while I have been out of the room has worked. He has got what he wants.

It is later on, after the IV is inserted, that the screaming starts. She is quiet at first but the noise coming from her gradually increases in pitch and volume like the wail of a siren. She looks wild. She is consumed by pain. The contractions that rack her body take hold of her at an ever-increasing speed. In between she lies back on the bed panting and exhausted.

There are various people all around her now, trying to get her to focus. They want her to sign the form that will give consent to have an epidural. They cannot give this pain numbing injection into her spinal column without her written consent. It will numb the contraction pain as well as all other feeling from the waist down. They hold her face in their hands talking loudly and try to snap her out of the moments of exhaustion that claim her completely.

Finally she consents, there is no fight left in her. The lioness has gone.

Hours later there is no clawing the walls. Anne-Marie is quietly strapped down with a belt across her belly to monitor baby's heartbeat. There are machines whirring with readouts and data on both sides of the bed. Her hand is taped up with a tube. Fluid is plop-plop-plopping through it, clear fluid that looks as innocent as water. Who would have guessed the havoc this substance created initially, causing her to go wild with pain and lose control? The nurses kindly put it in her bloodstream to bring on the contractions when we entered the hospital this morning, which seems like a lifetime ago.

When we arrived the contractions had slowed down, dried up like a desert stream under the stark hospital lights. The midwife suggested we all go home for a bit. But Anne-Marie was having none of it and insisted on staying at the hospital. Nothing prepared her for what would happen next.

I am amazed at how long she held out against the contractions as well as the staff. Larry is visibly relieved after the epidural is in place. He was so uncomfortable with the screaming. It totally interrupted his phone conversations.

When I came back in and the epidural was in place, Anne-Marie was lying on the bed, eyes closed. It had been a long night and everyone was tired. Larry left the room when he saw me enter. I am sat here next to her bed, with instructions to press the call button if any change happens.

Before he left Larry said something interesting about Anne-Marie. During her pregnancy she had heard a horrible birth story from a friend whose pregnancy had gone long past her due date and had to have her labour induced. Anne-Marie was terrified it would happen to her. She had been doing everything she could to start labour this past week, staying awake pacing the house the past couple of nights.

She was half-crazed from lack of sleep and worry on top of everything else. Even I am feeling the effects of not sleeping last night and the broken night before that. Who knows what inner torment she had been putting herself through these past days and long nights?

8pm. Baby was born two hours ago. He flopped onto the bed pale and weak but alive. I honestly had no idea how much could be done to a tiny baby in such a short time. There were masks and tubes and bright lights and little needles and rushing and bustle. The baby was crying. His thin arms flung out, wide fingers splayed.

I didn't know what to do, where to put myself, what to say. It was an intense time. I found myself standing against a wall looking over a sea of healthcare staff that washed in and out of the room like a human tide. I stood there feeling helpless during the actual moment of the birth. Anne-Marie lay on her back, her legs up in metal stirrups on either side of the bed. Her inner-most self was exposed for all to see. The doctor in charge, that young, rude, horrible doctor fumbled around with his instruments trying to pull the baby out. It felt like a violation and watching it was one of the hardest things I have ever done.

Even Larry looked pale and distant as he sat and watched what was happening to his wife. He held her hand but seemed to be wishing he was somewhere else. Looks of horror and disgust flashed over his face and were followed by morbid fascination at what was happening.

My heart went out to her lying there. I tried to hold her in my heart, hold all that was good and strong and true about her. I closed my eyes and inside my head told her how wonderful she was, how absolutely beautiful she was. When I opened them she was looking right at me from across the room, looking pale and washed out. I smiled, wanting to convey that I was still here, still holding onto her, still by her side. She closed her eyes again.

I cannot write everything that happened. I don't want to remember but the memory is burned into my brain. I wish I had looked away after that, but couldn't help staring at the brutality I witnessed. I feel weak and nauseas. I had no idea that birth could be this way.

Anne-Marie was taken into surgery after the birth as the tear to her insides was so big that it needed a lot of stitches. The doctor had made a little cut in her perineum just before the baby had been born to create a little extra space for the head. But the cut had split under the pressure of birth and grown much bigger. There had been a lot of blood.

After theatre Larry pushed Anne-Marie's wheel-chair (she wouldn't be walking for a while after the epidural and large tear) down to the neonatal ward. I didn't feel like I could follow them in and no-one invited me. So I have been waiting here in the corridor. But no one has come out.

It has been a long journey for all of us. The coming and going of hospital staff has all blurred together by now. I feel empty, sitting and staring at this wall as I wait. What do I do now? This wasn't on the birth plan. We never discussed what to do if things didn't go to plan. I'll just wait. I don't know how to get back to my car anyway. I left my wallet in the car along with my phone and iPod. So much for being organized.

Tuesday 23rd March

'What are you still doing here?' Larry threw the question at me as I sat outside the neonatal ward last night. He must have come out while my eyes were closed. He startled me.

I opened my mouth to answer but no answer came out. He was looking hostile and fraught at the same time. I felt intimated by him.

'How are they?' I asked, answering his question with a question of my own.

He shrugged and slid into the plastic seat next to mine. 'Suppose you need to get back for your car, don't you.' It was a statement not a question. He opened his wallet and pulled out some notes.

'Get a cab,' he said.

I stared at him in shock at the contempt and anger I felt directed at me. What had I done to deserve that kind of treatment? It felt like someone had punched me in the stomach, which was already hurting from the emotional roller-coaster ride of the past couple of days.

'Look,' he said, still staring at the wall, avoiding my eyes. 'She is everything I've got. It was my job to keep her safe and look how I failed her.'

To my utter surprise this man started to sob into his hands as they covered his face. It slowly dawned on me that actually he had been angry at himself, not me. I had been so wrapped up in my own story that I hadn't taken time to find out how he was. I had just assumed. I put my hand gently on his shoulder, not knowing what to say.

'It was horrible seeing her like that,' he said wiping his eyes. He looked tired and suddenly older. He stood up. 'I have to get back to her,' he said as he started walking away. He still hadn't looked at me.

Slowly I turned my head down to look at the money. Picking it up, I left that building of bustling uniforms, sanitary hand gel and security guards on the doors. I was glad to hand the money over to the first taxi driver I saw, who took me back to little Hengelwook and my patiently waiting car.

It felt like a lifetime ago I left it out there, so much has happened that it feels like the whole world has changed.

When I got in my car and sat behind the wheel, I realized I was still in shock. I was trying to remember how to drive when the housekeeper tapped on the window. I stared at her, trying to grasp the meaning of her words but for some reason I was having difficulty understanding her.

'The baby came this evening,' I managed to say eventually. She had been asking if the baby had been born. 'It's a little boy,' I finished, exhausted by saying the words. The housekeeper clapped her hands together and bustled off. I watched her as she disappeared into the house. Why was everyone moving so fast?

I drove slowly home, very slowly as I couldn't concentrate very well. I felt removed from my body and was having a hard time making it do what I wanted. At home, bed was an inviting sanctuary, a dark cave I crawled into.

I woke up hours later and I needed to write, to empty some of these words that were swimming around in my head. I feel like there is a numb, empty hole in my middle. Images from the hospital flash in front of my eyes and the events replay themselves over and over again.

I watched it rain in the weak light of a dismal day. The sky a uniform grey, big fat droplets of rain streak down the window while I lie on the bed. They remind me of the drops of blood I see when I close my eyes. Dreams were thick and full last night, nightmarish images of pale babies with long heads and eyes staring as I stood helplessly. I woke in a cold sweat. I don't like this.

Finally I got up and phoned Anne-Marie to ask how they were. It was surprising how shaky my voice was as I left a message on the answer machine. They will phone back if they want to talk to me.

Wednesday 24th March

It is still raining. I haven't heard from them; I hope they are okay. That baby was very pale. I guess I should be talking to my mentor about this. But I'm sure I'll be classified as a failure if anyone finds out how terribly this birth went. I feel like I should have known more about what to do. I should have done something to stop it from turning out that way. I should have been there but I felt like I was a million miles away as those needles went sticking in to her. I should have done something. I can't talk to anyone right now. I will stay in bed and listen to the rain hoping sleep will wipe the memory from my mind.

Thursday 25th March

More nightmares ~ this time they were about me. I was being dragged out of my soft warm bed towards a tunnel with a little light shining in. I could hear loud noises and I didn't want to go. I tried to scream and something filled my mouth. I woke up tangled in the bed covers, a sheet caught in my mouth as I gasped for air. It was 4 am when I looked at the clock.

Their baby was so still when he was dragged out I thought he was dead. The cord was wrapped around his body and there were lumps of black sticky stuff everywhere. It was only a snapshot, a couple of seconds until he was bundled up and whisked off to the station on the other side of the room to be sucked and masked until that first weak cry came a couple of long minutes later. Anne-Marie was calling out, 'My baby, my baby.' That snapshot has been ingrained in my mind and follows me around like a shadow. I run events over and over in my mind, but still feel numb and disconnected. Was there anything I could have done differently?

Friday 26th March

Numbness lifted a little today. I got out of bed and sat in the chair looking out over the bay watching the waves breaking and the birds gliding on the air currents. I still haven't heard from them. I am beginning to feel guilty. I was supposed to enhance the birth experience. Instead I was like a rabbit in the headlights faced with all that hospital intervention, all those people in uniforms and I froze. I felt useless and unqualified and wondered what on earth was I trying to do there? Who did I think I was?

Saturday 27th March

It's dark again now. Only a few nights ago I was sitting in the chair next to Anne-Marie's bed while she slept and everything appeared calm and quiet. I thought then that everything was going to be alright. The screaming and clawing before had shocked me but somehow I reasoned that the worst was behind and now everything was going to be okay.

Then things began to go wrong. But maybe I could have done something to change that. All those little niggling doubts I had during our antenatal meetings have been coming back to haunt me. The feelings I couldn't quite pinpoint, the lack of explanation about Larry's role, his open rudeness, the brushing off of any doubts. Looking back I see some serious issues we didn't address back then. I had no idea how important they would be in the end.

Sunday 28th March

It was the instruments that really affected me and are the subject of my nightmares. The tubes and wires and beeping monitors didn't shock me. I could somehow see past them, still see her lying there birthing her baby. It was when the doctor arrived, and Anne-Marie had her feet up in stirrups, that things started to feel strange, like I was going to faint. Not that blood normally bothers me. It was those instruments he took off the trolley, the one the nurse wheeled in after him, that made my eyes really widen.

I don't really know why but the feeling hit me deep in my stomach and I couldn't breathe properly. I was gasping for air. I tried to stay focused on what was happening but more and more people came in on the tide of bodies and pressed up against me. People stood around chatting about the most random things ~ TV programmes and car parking fines. There was a woman lying on her back and a man with those ghastly instruments and nobody even seemed to notice. I guess they must see it every day. But I felt dizzy and sick, unable to do anything but stand and watch.

I had another nightmare this afternoon while I was sleeping. There were voices yelling and someone was at the door with one of those instruments demanding to be let in.

'No, go away,' I yelled as I woke up scrambling from my bed. Everything was quiet, the curtains pulled closed against the afternoon grey sky.

Monday 29th March

Still they haven't called. Other people have been calling and texting, but I haven't bothered to answer. I don't know what to say. What do I tell people? 'Yeah, I went to a birth and I felt sick.' What kind of answer is that? I feel like a bad joke. Me, a Doula? Ha! Not likely.

The cats have been acting quite strange now as I look at them, all jumpy and skittish. They try to sit on my lap but I push them away. The whole world feels a long way away.

Tuesday 30th March

This time there was real thumping on the door, the cats jumped when they heard it too.

'Who is it?' I shouted at the closed door, my heart pounding.

'Me. Now open up,' came the unmistakable voice of my best friend in the world. My heart melted as I opened the door and looked out to see Jelly's friendly familiar face peering in at me.

They've all left now and although I'm alone again, things are quieter in my head. Looking back I'm not quite sure what happened to me this last week. All I have are the fragments written here in the diary and the images that have been bouncing around inside my head.

I got a shock when Jelly held the mirror up to my face in the bathroom earlier and I looked at myself for the first time in days. My eyes peered back at me from some place distant and empty. I saw lank dirty hair, black circles under the eyes tight with tension and stress oozing from every pore.

Who was I? What had I become? I stared at my reflection.

Nick had taken Valentina to the shops in the sling. I had hardly been aware of them when they had come in. Angelica took me to the bathroom and ran a deep hot bath, full of oils and herbs. She was like an angel.

I felt dazed and disorientated as she helped me undress and get into the bath. A flicker of a thought registered that it was slightly strange being naked in front of her but as soon as I stepped into the water I melted into relaxation and any questions disappeared. The warm water seeped into my bones and I breathed out, feeling layers of stress unwind. Jelly sat quietly on a stool and helped wash my hair. She scrubbed my back. She said very little and asked no questions, but her mind must have been burning with them.

Slowly I came back into my body, like waking up from a long enchanted sleep. I shook my head; the numbness was beginning to clear. I felt hungry. Delicious smells were drifting in from the kitchen

'Nick must have gotten back from the shops. Perhaps lunch is ready,' Angelica smiled as I sniffed the air.

Wrapped in warm towels, I dried myself then dressed quickly. I felt warm and clean. After the two bowls of delicious soup that Nick quietly passed me, I began to explain what had happened.

Once I had begun to talk I couldn't stop, the words just kept on coming and coming like a wall of water that had been held behind a dam. Along with the words came the emotions I had been unable to feel all this time. The numbness was replaced by emotion ~ by sadness, fear, distrust, anger.

Angelica and Nick sat across the table while I let this torrent of words wash out of the depths of me. They sat and listened, understanding my need to talk without being uninterrupted. Valentina, asleep in the other room, awoke at one point and Nick brought her in to breastfeed then took her away afterwards to settle.

I told them everything from the moment I got the first phone call. I spoke about the pre-birth meetings we had, the whole labour experience, the birth, leaving hospital and being here alone with my nightmares.

The story became clearer to me as I spoke. I began to see Larry's fear of the whole birth process from the beginning. How he used his phone to avoid being present with his wife because he couldn't or didn't know what to do. I saw how she lost her way even before we arrived at the hospital. Her fear of going overdue had created so much stress in her body even before labour had begun. I saw how the comments of the doctors and midwives had undermined her confidence and I could see the downward spiral of interventions that led to the outcome.

I had more perspective now. But still I couldn't understand why it had hit me so hard. Why had I suffered such shock at witnessing that birth? Everybody was alive and Anne-Marie and Larry had their baby. The nurses had been smiling; it was a successful birth according to the notes they wrote up. Was I the only one who felt deeply affected by the trauma I had witnessed?

My words finally dried up. Their story had been told; but what about my story? Why had I felt so numb afterwards? What had happened to me this last week when I totally shut down in shock?

We sat together watching the fire that Nick had lit in the wood burner, the flames licking the logs yellow and orange. I am beginning to feel alive again.

Wednesday 31st March

A dream shocked me into consciousness this morning. I laid wide eyed in my dark room replaying the scenes over in my mind. In the dream a dog was giving birth. She lay panting, flopped on the floor. The first puppy came out and began wriggling around as she licked it. The second puppy was stillborn and after sniffing it mama dog pushed it away. The third puppy got stuck with only its head sticking out. I found my hands helping to gently ease its shoulders out, followed by the rest of its body. Mama dog sniffed but didn't lick it clean and didn't help it snuffle its way to the teat. She almost rolled her eyes and suffered its presence uncomfortably. I held the stillborn pup in my hand, wrapped it in a clean piece of cloth then buried it under a tree outside, feeling hot tears roll down my cheeks as I did so. Then I went back and held the third puppy that had been rejected.

I woke up crying, the pillow was wet. I stripped the bedclothes and realized it was a bright sunny day outside. The dream had given me a chance to grieve and release a feeling that needed to come out. I had learned of my dead sister one day from my Grandpa, but there wasn't much to tell. She died before she was born and was never spoken of again. A year later I came along, but the pregnancy wasn't given much importance. I was that third puppy, I was the rejected child. My mother would not or could not love me as she loved her first-born and her second child had died in her womb. Maybe my mother had lost her maternal instinct through unresolved grief. I don't know what happened, the past is a mystery. There are so many untold stories, jigsaw pieces floating around. I feel reconnected to the grief of losing a sister I never knew. The tears were hot while they fell but when they dried up I felt lighter inside.

Later I phoned my mentor Leanne and debriefed Anne-Marie's birth experience with her. She listened attentively then asked questions which made me look back over what happened and link things together.

I saw how my intuition had been trying to tell me things from the beginning but I had brushed it aside. I had wondered why I had never met Larry before the day of labour and why his role had not been really discussed. What things were unspoken but still present? I saw the huge amount of issues that had been going on under the surface as I spoke with Leanne about how birth brings things into the open. Their relationship had issues, he wasn't (or wasn't able to be) there for her emotionally and she was desperately screaming at him to be present with her.

Then we looked at my reaction to the things that happened, being bustled out of the house and into a role I wasn't comfortable with. Also being side-lined and ignored in the hospital. I could see the lack of personal respect I felt and the helplessness I experienced watching Anne-Marie struggle. The biggest shock was the moment of birth. Every time I've tried to explain about those instruments I find my voice cracking, without really understanding why.

Leanne gently prodded, 'Tell me about your birth, Joy.' I felt tears spring into my eyes, well up and cascade down my face.

'I can't,' I managed to squeeze out of my tight throat. 'My mother won't tell me and my father...I don't know where he is, or even if he is alive.'

I felt more tears roll down as the waves of emptiness washed over me. I wasn't drowning anymore but allowing the emotion to move through me. This was so much harder than when we spoke about our births during the training weekend. It all felt so raw now and so much more present after what I had witnessed.

I could hear Leanne on the other end of the phone making soothing noises as she heard the expression of my heart, of the pain and emptiness. How did I enter this world? Why was I crying so much? What are my beliefs about who I am? I remembered my dream about the enchanted rope. What do I believe that is no longer true?

I have somehow been taught to believe that birth is hard, painful work. It is a bloody, messy emergency requiring flashing lights and rushing doctors in gowns. I have images in my head of a woman clutching her belly while being wheeled into a hospital room. Her white-faced husband is running alongside holding her hand while gowned medical professionals attend to the business of delivering the baby. Birth is medical, dangerous and frightening, something to be trusted only to the professionals as a woman's body cannot to do it alone. There is so much fear around birth. Not necessarily my own fear, more like a cultural fear. But it was out of my own surprised mouth that those images poured.

Birth is mysterious. It is something that happens behind closed doors. A hospital birth is the norm in this country, home birth for the minority. I wonder how I have come to learn about this culture of fear around birth.

My teachers are all around me, I guess. The births on the television are often dramatic and full of emergencies. There are stories about birth on the news, about people giving birth on planes or in taxis because they couldn't get to the hospital in time. Birth stories passed around mouth to mouth, the more gruesome the better to remember them by.

So is this is my cultural programming, my birth culture? What about me, what do I feel about birth? That birth culture might have been what I have grown up with and see all around me but it doesn't mean that I believe all of it. Lots of what I did believe has also been challenged by Valentina's birth.

Birth is something natural. That is what I feel to be true. The body has grown this child for nine months; surely it also has the capacity to give birth? What are we so afraid of? Why all this fear? Is it fear of pain, death or loss of control?

~ April ~

Thursday 1st April

I phoned Mother today. My resolve was firmly set as I picked up the receiver. After saying hello, I asked to hear my birth story. The line went quiet.

'What's this, April fools?' she twittered, like she had already been on the sherry.

I asked again, 'Can you please tell me the story of my birth. I would really like to know how I was born.'

She fumbled through a list of excuses. I swear she has them written in a list next to the phone to reel off in any given situation.

'It was too long ago. It's not important. You're alive, aren't you? Can't you just be grateful for that? Why do you need to upset me by digging around in the past?'

Again I insisted, 'Mother, I would really like to know and you're the only person able to tell me.'

Then she said something that took the breath out of my lungs. I don't know what prompted her to say it ~ maybe I had made her mad or maybe she was fed up with the questions fired at her.

For whatever reason she replied, 'I wasn't the only person there who would remember. Your father was also present. He'll tell it like it was, if you can find him.'

My father! My father would tell me? My father was alive? My father knew my birth story? I had a father!

My mind raced. Questions mounted up in my head, scrambling over each other in their eagerness to get out of my mouth and find their respective answers. But silence was my only response, the breath momentarily absent from my lungs, my mouth open and eyes wide.

Mother went on, 'Yes, your father, if he hasn't gone to hell yet, would tell you every last detail and probably enjoy telling it, curse his soul. No, don't ask me where he is. I heard neither hide nor hair since the day he walked out the door. So don't go asking for that story neither, because there's nothing telling there.'

I was stunned. My mother cursing my father was nothing new to me. But the possibility that he may still be alive was incredible. He could hold a piece to the puzzle that is my life.

Putting the phone down, I was racked with unimagined fears. What could I do now? I wanted to find him yet at the same time was terrified of hearing his story and of being rejected again.

I used to wonder about him when I was a child, this mystery man. Who was he, where was he, would he swoop in one day and rescue me? But as the years passed and nothing ever came of this person the dream faded. The desire to know him shrank and shrivelled. Who did he think he was anyway? I became mad at him and in turn rejected even the idea of him.

My grandpa was more like a father to me than anyone who turned up now could ever be. When grandpa died, I let the memory of wanting a father die along with him. That had been so long ago I had almost forgotten I had a father until recent events took down the memory from a dusty shelf in a forgotten corner of my mind.

Friday 2nd April

I needed a day to clear my head because of all the internal work that has been going on. I needed to feel the muscles in my body, the air in my lungs and the ground under my feet. I needed to feel my humanness.

The air was crisp and clear at the allotments; people were friendly, heads popping up as I walked past, hands waving, nods and smiles.

Arriving at my patch was sad. I saw how much time had passed. I hadn't been up since the big storm which was the day before Anne-Marie gave birth. There was a lot of storm damage where the high winds had snapped branches and whipped things around. The bamboo wigwam for the beans was totally destroyed. The cabbage, carrots and peas were alive under cloches, but not very happy. The greenhouse seedlings had not survived so long on their own and had shrivelled up to nothing.

Like sleeping beauty I have awoken to find that time has passed without my knowing. It feels like I have been cheated out of time. Lost in my dark dreams it slipped me by. I am still waking up, feeling a bit dazed, realizing that my presence is not required for the world to keep on turning.

There were so many questions I tried not to think about while I set to getting things back into shape by preparing new beds to be sown, clearing away and tidying up. The other allotment people were friendly but no one came over to ask where I'd been.

They just called over things like, 'Good to see you up here.' It felt like they were wary. Maybe they could see the lines of stress still etched into my face. Could they sense the cloud I had been lost beneath still trailing me like a bad smell? I threw myself into the land and let my worries dissolve like the clumps of earth on the end of my fork.

Coming home to a hot bath eased the tension from my bones. I had invited Angelica and Nick over to share some food together this evening. It was my way of saying thank you for bringing me out of the darkness and back into the light.

I don't call her Jelly any longer. The strength and love she had shown me after the trauma of Anne-Marie's birth had changed the way I saw my best friend. She is an angel, and her name is Angelica. I hope everyone can have a friend like her to share both the highs and the lows.

Angelica told me how Hilary has been asking after me. They cross paths often, in the park or on the beach walking their dogs, always stopping to say hello.

I don't know what to do with the information mother told me yesterday about my father. Angelica seemed worried about my delving too deeply too quickly and part of me agrees. My whole life has been fatherless and now suddenly I might have a father. I don't feel like I need to rush out and find him, a few more days, weeks or months will give me time to accept it.

Part of me feels confused and angry that he could walk out on his wife and two children. Another part of me feels sad for him. He missed out on being a father. Where was he? What was he doing?

I guess part of me realizes I always knew I could have looked for him before, but never bothered, not knowing what to say or what I would want from him anyway. Now at least he has something that I want, he has knowledge of me, of my entry into the world. Surprisingly I feel a compassion I didn't really know I could feel while still feeling angry and hurt at the same time. It is discovering a fuller spectrum of emotions, like I have discovered a whole new section of colours to paint with.

Saturday 3rd April

With a full feeling in my belly this morning, I woke feeling more grounded. Like a dog with a bone I needed to call my mother again, to get something more from her.

Instead of asking how I was born, I asked something else that has always mystified me, 'Why did you call me Joy?'

As a child I was made to feel ugly and unwanted. I bore the brunt of harsh words. My older brother managed to keep out of the way better than I did but I could not justify why I always felt so discriminated against. She would use my name almost as a weapon.

'Joy,' she would half sneer, half command as if the words were a contradiction in terms.

There was no joy in her being, or in her life, just me with this name that felt heavy and encumbering. Why had she named me so?

I had asked half expecting a similar response to the day before yesterday. I didn't care so much anymore for her harshness no longer cut me like it once did. I was past that now.

Something was different about her today. Maybe she had been thinking about it since Thursday. Maybe she hadn't been at the sherry yet today. Maybe she was just tired of holding it in. For whatever reason she decided to answer the question, and not with the scathing tone of the other day but the resigned voice of one who has had enough. It went something like this:

'You wanna know why you were called Joy? Ha, that's finally a decent question young lady. That is, it took you a while, didn't it? Instead of parroting off the same old ones...blah blah. Misery would've been more like it, eh? It was them nurses that did it, I blame them. Didn't force me mind, nobody goes around forcing me to do anything. They just kept on, didn't they.'

Then mother put on this high pitched whiny kind of voice, which I guessed was supposed to be the tone the nurses had used.

'Oh, just look at 'er, little bundle of joy she is, perfect little thing. Look at these little fingers here, look at your little joy.'

'And there I was trussed up in that hospital bed, not eating, not sleeping for days, just suffering to high heaven from the shock of it all and them there nurses would poke you into my lap all bundled up and try to get you to feed. And there I was not even speaking in those days as from where I saw it there wasn't anything worth saying any more so I just sat there not caring about a soul in the world, not really hearing what them nurses were whittering on about. Only that last word seemed to come through and I remember I looks at them and I says 'Joy?' not understanding what they were saying or their smiling.

'Yes, lurvie,' one nurse said, 'there's your joy,' and pointed to you.

All I saw was the pink blanket laying on my lap, then they pulls the top down and I sees your little face feeding and I turns to the nurses an asks again, 'Joy?'

But they must have taken it as a sign, superstitious lot them nurses, seems I hadn't been speaking much since, you know, so from then on every time they brought you over to me from the nursery they'd say,

'Here you go lurvie, here's your little Joy.'

I didn't bother to correct them then. Then one day the registrar came around he says the time is running out for me to register the birth and what was your name, it was them that said it really, them nurses.

'Oh yes, Mr Registrar, that's little Joy Thorpe there,' and they gave him my name and your father's name, curse his soul, and there it was on the certificate before I knew it, it was done.

I didn't have any name for you, couldn't even have told you my own name, I reckon, in those days what with the shock of it all. Wasn't ready for you was we, didn't even have a pram, had to borrow one from Mrs McCarthy down the way. Mind you, it was a long time 'til we went home, I just wasn't right after it all, the shock of it. I never forgave your father for that, may his bones rot, good thing I never laid eyes on him again, I say.'

Then she stopped this monologue abruptly almost as if realizing just how much she had said. She made a quick excuse and put the phone down before I had a chance to say another word.

I've written all this down as quickly as possible before the words dry up in my memory. There was so much to listen to. She had inadvertently told me what had happened after my birth.

Mother had suffered from shock post-partum. Shock so bad she had to stay in hospital until the time to register my birth was nearly up. I knew there were six weeks to register. Had she been in that state for so long?

Had she been in the same hospital all that time? My father had been there at my birth but had left and was never seen again. My name was an accident given to me by a nurse who was just trying to get my mother to look at me. The name stuck because my mother wasn't able to think of another one. I feel dizzy sitting here realizing this. Still it does begin to make sense, the way she treated me during my childhood, the way she used my name.

I tried to listen while mother spoke today, without the floodgates of emotion ripping open and deafening my ears to hearing her actual words.

But now as I write the tears come, dripping down my face making dark splotches on the paper. It isn't a roar of anger or rage at my mother, but a kind of hollow emptiness, which is funny because I just learnt more about my beginning than I ever knew before.

The sadness of the woman who is my mother touches me and I feel for her suffering. After giving birth, her husband left her and she was so traumatized she no longer recognized her own baby.

Whatever negative character traits my mother has and suffers from, she is still a human being and I have never been more aware of her humanness than I am today. For maybe the first time in my life I feel compassion towards her.

Sunday 4th April

Compassion: noun~ a feeling of deep sympathy and sorrow for another who is suffering or stricken by misfortune, accompanied by a strong desire to help them.

Maybe compassion is the wrong word because I don't feel like I have a strong desire to help either of my parents. But I do feel more sympathy towards them now than I ever have before, now I know more about what happened.

Monday 5th April

There he was on the screen in black and white: my father. Well, his name was there along with his home town, email and a photo.

I'm not really sure why I went looking for him, probably curiosity. I typed his name into the Facebook search, just to see how many men called Harold Benjamin Thorpe there were in the world. There was only one person with that exact name. I sat looking at his photo on the screen. It was a close-up of a face, just his eyes, nose and mouth. The more I looked the more I could see the face of my older brother looking back at me.

'Dad,' I whispered to the computer screen and the word sounded like a foreign language.

Putting a face to a name I had never used. Other information was minimal, just an email address.

Despite the ringing in my ears I pulled up my email account and started typing. I needed to release the words that were mounting inside me. I wrote and wrote and asked why.

Why did you leave when I was born?

Why did you never contact your children?

Why did you just disappear?

Why did you walk away?

Why?

Why?

Then I clicked send. It was like a slip of the mouse rather than an intentional decision to contact my father. But it was done.

I left the house straight away after that. Walked the beach, walked the park, seeing nobody and nothing really, just totally engrossed in the world in my head. It is a world of turbulence and unknowns. Coming home, I couldn't even turn the computer back on for fear that he might actually have responded. I went to bed instead.

Tuesday 6th April

Some of the missed phone calls from last week were from the art gallery. Apparently my work has been selling so well they needed more prints and would like to talk about my new pieces.

I phoned briefly to say I wasn't really focusing on work, but yes, I did have some new pieces they could have. I didn't really want to go into deep discussions and negotiations about it all. But they were surprisingly easy to deal with for once, and seemed so happy to hear from me.

This is my income, after all, and I need to keep them on my side so I agreed to see them. They promised to sort out all the prints and would come around and see my pieces in my studio without me having to lug them over to the gallery. This was a turnaround.

They arrived within the hour at my workshop. I said from the start that I wasn't negotiating today. I had no energy or time to engage in it.

I flung out an outrageous price tag on the three pieces of work I had ready to go ~ the one of the gulls flying low in the stormy sky, and the two experimental ones with balanced stones suggesting pregnant women. I was expecting them to laugh at the cost.

It came as a total shock when they just agreed to pay and asked, would they be able to take them today if the payment went into my account as cash?

I stared at them. I realized they must have taken this as a negative indication for they pulled out some cash.

What was going on? I used to have to haggle to get a half decent price from them, now they were coming to me and not even blinking an eyelid at outrageous price tags. It was unbelievable.

Then the story came out and I understood why I was getting the red carpet treatment. A photographer from a big glossy magazine had been in town. He had taken shots of the street with the gallery in with one of my big pieces in the window. That photo of the street, which is an idyllic cobbled flower-filled wonder that just invites you to stroll down, had made the front page. My painting was fully visible in the photo. It caught the eye of a column writer who had turned up and bought it straight out of the gallery's window. He had taken the story up in his column, writing about his latest art find. Now prints had been pouring off the shelves as quickly as the gallery could stock them, their overall sales had rocketed and business was booming.

My name had been dripping from columns the glossy magazine world over and now people wanted to buy more. I had to sit down. Nothing had prepared me for this. I had been off the face of the planet for a couple of weeks and look at what had happened in my absence.

They took the work I had ready. Asked me please to keep working, they would collect everything I produced and would pay what I asked. They were talking about a whole range ~ tea towels, mugs, coasters, T shirts, mouse pads as well as the already-running greeting cards and wall prints. All I could think about when I closed the door behind them was my father. He was like a fog in front of my eyes. I still didn't turn on the computer though. Not yet.

Wednesday 7th April

I got the email today and read it with hands shaking on the keyboard. My father, Ben, as he called himself, had replied.

It wasn't anything like I could have imagined. It was as full of feeling and emotion as my mother is void of it. As I read on my eyes filled with tears. As I read his side to the story it was as if he was here in the room talking to me. I could almost hear his voice filling my ears, full of sadness. He wrote about the years of wanting to contact us, my brother and me. He had suffered from an inner struggle, not knowing if we would accept him or want to hear from him after he had walked out.

He wrote the story of my birth. Reading it horrified me and at the same time laid to rest demons that had plagued me these past days and weeks.

The nightmares I had after Anne-Marie's birth made sense now. I could see how her birth had triggered a deep memory within me. My own birth had been traumatic.

He had watched my mother be drugged and cut wide open. Silently he watched as I was ripped out with huge metal tongs that had made my head an unnatural shape. He thought he had spawned a devil and guilt ripped him apart.

He had stumbled out of the delivery room onto the streets and never returned. He spent years living on the streets, his sleep tormented by inner demons. He had suffered from both drug addiction and mental illness.

Then a homelessness charity found him and took him into their care. They helped him to clean up, counselled him and he found his way again.

But by that time he felt unable to contact us again for fear of rejection. The fact that he had a family out there somewhere was like ancient history to him, he knew it had happened but the details were not clear. His brain had been affected in ways hard to understand rationally. So he took a job in a software firm, and threw himself into work day and night, developing software at the time when business was booming.

Fortune smiled on him. He became successful in business. He made a fortune in software, then sold up and retired early. Now he did a bit writing for magazines columns, mainly for pleasure rather than necessity.

As I continued to read, my mouth hung open. He wrote that he had recently seen a street photo on the desk of a co-writer in the magazine. There was an art gallery in the street with a piece of work in the window that enraptured him. He travelled to this town and bought this piece, arranging to have it shipped home.

Only when it arrived a week later did he notice that the artist was called Joy Thorpe. At first he thought the surname was merely a coincidence. He didn't know his lost daughter's first name. The next day my email had arrived.

Thursday 8th April

I woke before the sun this morning. Lying in bed feeling the cool sea air drifting in the open window, I felt like I had travelled to another place, another universe parallel to my old one yet significantly different.

Finally I got up; made a pot of fresh tea from herbs Angelica had brought around yesterday evening. Her sense of timing never ceases to amaze me. She just happened to be passing last night after I had received the email, just happened to have a bunch of herbs in her arms for calming and soothing.

She looked into my face as I opened the door.

'Thought you might like to share a cuppa,' she smiled at me.

How does she do it? Just coincidence you could say.

My brain was already trying to accept the incredible coincidence that had happened with my father. What with my painting and the gallery and his magazine and

~ 122 ~

the whole timing of it. I was looking for firm ground to stand on. I was in a whirlwind.

The story poured out onto the kitchen table like a rare sweet honey. Angelica lapped up every word with an open mouth.

For the first time in my entire adult life I realized that I do not feel like an orphan. Not that I had been aware that was how I felt. But perspective is an interesting thing and it had changed sides.

However I am not fully onto the other side quite yet. There is still a long way to go before I can get to know this person who has been foreign to me my whole life. There are still wounds that need healing. That first contact was unlike anything I could have imagined. If I believed in a god, I would say she was having a divine joke with me.

Today I need to get my hands in the soil and around rock, to feel the elemental forces at work, to ground myself. I need to work physically to move away from this infernal dialogue inside my head about Ben and my childhood and old hurts surfacing. I don't want to think, I just want to do. Writing this down helps to shift things but today I also want to create something.

10 pm. What a day for creation! The allotment was so dry not much was done, merely some watering and compost churning, which felt quite a lot like what my mind was doing ~ turning things over. But the real beauty started to happen once I got to the beach.

It was a stunning afternoon. The light was perfect, it got richer and deeper and lusher as the afternoon wore on. The rocks were also amazing. They just seemed to spring out from the beach into my hands telling me where they wanted to go.

I balanced rocks upon rocks, making stacks of three or four at a time. The more difficult the balances, the more improbable the angles, the more they appealed to my sense of creation. I didn't know what was going to happen until the stones balanced themselves.

A woman was the first to appear in stone, her frame tall and strong yet most definitely a woman for her curves. Next to her another woman was born, again tall and strong but this time she was swollen with child and the two women stood together a long time.

I took photos to work on turning them into paintings another day. Then another form came out of the rock. I write it like that because although it was my hands moving the rocks it really felt like those rocks spoke to my hands and told them where they wanted to go. My hands just needed to listen. My mind was thankfully quiet while I worked.

Another woman appeared then another and another until finally there was an entire circle of rock women standing against the backdrop of sea and sky. They were my elemental women. I felt awed by their presence. I sat with them. My hands were aching but my spirit was satisfied.

For some reason it was particularly quiet on that part of the beach. Hardly anyone came by and nobody spoke to me at all for the entire afternoon, though some people seemed to be watching from a distance.

Then right at the end of the day as the sun was setting and I sat drinking my final cup of tea from the lukewarm flask, Hilary came by.

We sat together for what felt like an age without speaking, just looking at the ring of elemental women. It was the first time I had seen her since, well since before Anne-Marie's birth. There seemed no words to say. But that was okay. She seemed to know and didn't ask but just accepted me as I was without question. We just sat in companionable silence with the circle of elemental women. It was perfect.

Friday 9th April

Tonight I spoke to my father for the first time in my life. He had asked me for my phone number when he emailed but I couldn't give it to him straight away.

It felt like the hardest thing I could do, to allow this person into my life and open my heart to being vulnerable. Then I realized that it was exactly what I needed to do.

When the phone rang I didn't think. I just grabbed it.

'Hello Joy, it's Ben,' he said. My heart leapt up into my throat and I could not find any words to say. I felt hot prickles in the back of my eyes as my throat tightened and my chest stiffened. I could feel my old response ~ wanting to close off from the pain, wanting to turn away, to get as far as possible from this feeling that was so uncomfortable.

But this time, instead of running I turned towards it. Towards this feeling I had been so afraid of, had been running from, in fact, as long as I could remember. The pain of hurt and separation and loss and abandonment hit me in the chest. I turned towards it and opened my arms to let the enormity of what was happening wash over me like a wave. I stopped worrying about whether

I were going to drown in the tide of emotion and instead just let it be.

As I did this, with my father on the other end of the phone, something happened I wasn't expecting. I didn't drown. I didn't go under this flood let loose from its gates. I cried and cried. He was there listening, not saying much but I could tell he was listening, crying himself as well.

I spoke about how it felt to be fatherless all my life. Letting the words pour from my tongue without censoring whether they were appropriate, just letting it all roll out.

It felt like I was on the knife-edge of life itself, intensely alive and more in touch with how I actually felt than I had ever been before.

He asked if I would like to meet up one day and I said yes. My fatherless life is over. Wherever this goes from here, I now know the story of my father. We cannot recapture those lost years but only be open to receive what is on offer now.

Saturday 10th April

Life can be a mystery sometimes. I woke up this morning to the dawn chorus and lay in bed feeling the lightness of my being as my body seemed to hum in time with the vibrant celebration that was happening all around me. I pulled open the curtains and was witness to the often unseen light show happening in the early morning sky and watched the unseen painter slashing the clouds red and golden.

Feeling like a deep transformation had happened in the dark place I had just come from. I could do nothing but sit and cry. But this time it wasn't those heavy splashing tears that had been falling but ones that fell almost unnoticed and from a different place in my heart, a place of gratitude and humbleness. Looking back at my journey with Anne-Marie, I felt compassion instead of remorse and could sit and allow the emotion to fill me without needing to justify any of it, to just let it be.

After breakfast I phoned Anne-Marie. The maid answered and after a while the lady of the house came to the phone. She sounded tired but OK and I arranged to pop over later.

I took flowers and a basket of spa things for pampering. We spent the morning together. Larry had gone back to work and we had time to talk.

The baby was beautiful, a blonde buff of hair perched on top of his head. We talked of the practical things of mothering, of which I realized I had a lot to learn as I listened to her talk. I had taken a list of local groups for her, the peer breastfeeding support group I had heard wonderful things about and other groups for mums with new-borns.

Then she went very quiet, sitting with her hands in her lap, looking down at them. It was my turn to speak.

I shared her birth story from my perspective. I shared how I had seen it, not the harrowing account that had become a nightmare but the strength I had seen in her, the lioness that had roared.

And as I spoke I could see some dignity and strength of character return to her slumped shoulders as she sat up a little straighter in the chair. She looked me in the eye at first almost in disbelief then in self recognition. She had been all of those things.

So things had not gone as written in her birth plan and there had been lots of strong emotions but it had been quite a learning experience. She warmed to the subject and we began in earnest discussing what had happened, looking at how things had gone down that route and what an opportunity for learning it had been. There was still raw emotion there and at times the tears rolled down our faces.

I felt able now to be with this outpouring, to see it for what it was, like a cloud on the blue sky that came for a while then passed on. By acknowledging the presence of the feeling and not trying to ignore it but expressing it and then letting it drift on by. How healing that was. We said our goodbyes a lot lighter and clearer.

I won't be doing any more postnatal visits. She has a lot of help at home. She did say that if she gets pregnant again I will be her first choice as Doula, which really touched me in the most heartfelt way. As I drove away, I looked at the clear blue sky and saw it as a reflection of the clarity that I was feeling.

The allotment called me on the way home. I worked feeling grounded and like life was on the move again. The sun was surprisingly hot so I put on the cap that had always hung on the nail but had never been worn.

Sunday 11th April

Angelica and I spent an indulgent day at the Spa. We took a sauna and swam. Then we met up with her family and all went out for dinner at the fabulous Italian restaurant. This was followed by live music at The

Barn, where I danced till my feet couldn't move any longer. The music was good. It felt wonderful to shake and let my body move.

Monday 12th April

Wow! A surprise email from Leanne came today. 'Doula needed' was the subject line.

I opened it and read on. Leanne had just been contacted by a woman who was thirty six weeks pregnant and looking for a birth Doula.

This woman was geographically closer to me than Leanne. She lived in the same town as me.

Leanne wondered how I was doing. She realized it was quite soon after my last birth and didn't want to overload me with something if I felt I couldn't be present for someone else. I could say no and that would be fine. She would also be happy to be my back-up Doula if I were to take on the job.

She also wrote that this would be my second attended birth as a trainee Doula. Providing that I finished my other written assignments and kept up with the required readings I would soon be a qualified Doula. A qualified Doula! That sent shivers down my spine.

I was nearly there, and part of me didn't feel ready. But I recognized that dark part of me. It was the same negative voice that told me my art was nothing more than a child's scribbling even though it sold through a professional gallery. It was that same negative voice that told me the new dress I bought or new idea I had was just no good. That voice was intent on stopping me from achieving anything worthwhile or feeling good about myself. It is my inner critic. It is my shadow side that I have to consciously choose not to listen to. I turn my back on it now as I trained myself to do during art school in order to be able to push myself further than the limits of what I believed possible. To turn away from the darkness and to see the light of faith, of belief in myself and accepting that maybe I could do this seemingly massive thing laid out in front of me. I could do it, I was good enough, and I was capable. That, too, was scary. To think that I could be what I wished to be. I took a deep breath and continued reading.

I read what Leanne knew about the situation. The woman and her partner had been taking antenatal classes with Leanne and were keen to have a home water birth.

The woman was a dancer and in good shape physically. Her partner was supportive and loving. My role would be to support the pair of them rather than be the primary support.

Leanne wrote about how all births were different and of the importance of not painting them all with the same brush. She mentioned something else that struck me. She wrote that how we are born can affect our whole life. I could see the difference between how Valentina and Anne-Marie's baby came into the world. Could this really affect their whole lives? Was birthing really that important? If this was true, surely the medical profession would be doing everything they could to make birth the best day of our lives.

This new situation already felt different to my previous experience. I was interested to meet this new couple, to have a different experience. Also, having Leanne involved felt good. I wrote back saying that I would be happy to meet with them. Then we would decide if we wanted to work together.

This time it feels different. Like being involved with this family is an option and I am able to decide if I want to do it. So different from the need and urgency I felt with Anne-Marie. Even though this woman is quite far along in her pregnancy and theoretically I could be on call in a couple of weeks, it still feels like I could be ready. We will see.

I met Hilary and her dogs on the beach afterwards and we sat on a bench watching the sea together. I shared some of my personal journey with her about the last couple of weeks and she listened quietly.

When I had poured it all out she smiled and said I was a marvel. I grinned at this, not feeling marvellous at all. She said that I had allowed the situation to teach me in a way that no amount of book learning could ever do and this had opened the way to personal transformation. This cracking open of the heart was a way to get the blood flowing again.

She said that our conditioned response to emotional pain is to draw back from it, to close up and hope it goes away. But by opening to the experience and allowing ourselves to feel it fully in the moment we can use it to clear away old patterns and conditioned responses. Her outlook seemed to come from a very Buddhist perspective as she spoke of the impermanence of things and how by allowing ourselves to flow with it, we were in fact engaging more fully with life itself. I love our ability to share to this depth.

The years have given her great gifts, not all of them easy or pleasant. But the real gems, she said come with reflection and opening to life in all its glory. She praised me for being brave enough to accept the path I have chosen with all its troughs and peaks. Evidence of this was my openness to take on another client, knowing what I now know, having been freed from the ignorance of inexperience. I pray for more courage to be braver still.

Tuesday 13th April

I am going to meet the new couple on Thursday evening at their home here in town. Leanne is in town that day for another appointment and I invited her to have lunch with me before I go over to meet them. This way I get to debrief some more with her in person, which is an added bonus.

This afternoon I went along to the peer breastfeeding support group at the local health centre. After having recommended it to Anne-Marie I felt like it would be a good idea to pop in and see what was going on there.

A lovely lady met me and introduced me to the open group that meets once a week. The room was full of mamas and babies, some just a few days old, others beginning to crawl, while older siblings played with toys in an adjoining room.

I had heard about how many mums give up breastfeeding because it hurts or because the baby isn't gaining weight. But these issues can be easily remedied with the right support.

It was shocking to hear that ninety per cent of women in our country give up breastfeeding in the first six weeks. Without the right support or information, it becomes an insurmountable struggle and many women give up without really wanting to.

The early days of adjusting to life with a new baby is probably one of the most physically challenging times of any woman's life. Added to that, the hormonal readjustment the body goes through from pregnancy to motherhood is enormous.

How did these women do it? I wondered as I looked around the room and saw smiling women and cooing babies amid cups of tea and slices of cake. The women told me about the importance of making sleep a priority in the early days. That meant ignoring the housework and piles of unwashed dishes. Some had set up food chains and wish lists so if people wanted to come and visit the new family they had to bring some food and lend a hand doing a load of dishes or some laundry. This also limited the amount of visitors and the inclination of the mother to act as a hostess.

Being open to being vulnerable had turned into something that empowered them and helped the whole process of adjustment flow much more easily.

These women also usually hold their babies and breastfeed them often. The peer supporters said that both of these things helped the production of soothing hormones, which in turn facilitated the milk let-down reflex. Night feeding is also an important part of the puzzle as not only is a new-born stomach capacity the same size as a small marble and digests milk quickly, but the major milk production hormones are most active during the night. So lots of rest during the day is vital.

The support group gave these women strength by being with other mums who had also made the decision to breastfeed despite what well-meaning relatives might be saying.

We spoke about previous generations who had been given different information about the benefits of breastfeeding versus bottle feeding and had done what they thought best at the time.

'We know now that breast milk is simply the very best thing for babies,' one of the peer supporters told me. She also happened to be pregnant herself.

'It has a unique role in providing the best nutritional and immunological start to a child's life, being made specifically every day to provide exactly what each baby needs.'

She told me the incredible fact that glands around mama's nipple take in bacteria from the baby's mouth. Then mama's body makes antibodies using her own immune system, which were then given to the baby via milk.

She was on a roll now. I could see her eyes light up as she realized she had found someone genuinely interested in the benefits of breastfeeding. She reeled off statistics about some of the advantages for mothers like a waitress reading the daily specials. If a woman breastfeeds for over three months then breast cancer is three times less likely (as well as in their daughters), osteoporosis is three times less likely and ovarian cancer half as likely. It also helps lose weight gained in pregnancy, up to five hundred calories a day.

For baby, the benefits are also awe-inspiring: less risk of chest infections, food allergies, gastroenteritis, eczema, asthma, cot death , urinary tract infections, ear infections, obesity in later life, lower risk of heart disease as an adult and (this was probably my favourite one) likely to have higher than average scores on intelligence tests in later life.

'So can everyone breastfeed?' I asked. 'I mean, when faced with that huge list of benefits, why would anyone not want to do it?'

The answer was complicated and multi-layered. It included cultural pressures about being a liberated woman and not a baby slave. This idea began as propaganda during the Second World War, the generations of our grandparents and great grand-parents who handed the idea down. There also was the controversial topic of the advertising of infant formula.

From earlier conversations, I knew that other factors included physical pain and on-going lack of support due to ignorance of the mechanics of breastfeeding. The peer supporters told me that occasionally there are real reasons to give up breastfeeding but that is only the case in about two per cent of mothers, due to illness or biological reasons.

I left the group with my belly full of cake and my head full of facts. Walking home, I seemed to see formula adverts everywhere.

Wednesday 14th April

It was a wet, grey day today, perfect for being in the workshop. The gallery loved the new images and is running with the whole thing. It's funny. Before I might have been absorbed in the whole marketing process to get into magazines and promote the whole line. But life has changed so much these past few weeks and my priorities have shifted enormously.

In a way, life has taken over and I feel content to sit back and let things flow. I don't need to do anything about it. The gallery is more than happy to be in charge.

Its better this way as I just get to do the fun bit of creating and not deal with the details of business negotiation.

Dreams of flying like a bird came last night, the effortless gliding felt free and easy. I spent the day using the workshop as a therapeutic outlet. I used colours selected at random, not with any purpose in mind, but just to express how I was feeling and let them explode over the paper. This was not exactly a pretty sight but not ugly either. It didn't matter as it wasn't for anyone but me. I let my soul fly like the birds of my dreams and let go of preconceived notions of what art was.

It was like looking into the art gallery of my soul. The depth of my confusion changed from trepidation to knowledge then into understanding followed by forgiveness. I covered page after page with colour explosions. At first they were dark and swirling, full of confusion but little by little the colours calmed down and the pages began to be less busy until finally the last one that left my hands was simple, mainly white with just a single sweep of pink swirling around in a peaceful kind of fashion. It looked like a woman holding a woman holding a baby.

By the time I had allowed all the colours their full expression it was dusk outside so I went out for a quick walk along the beach.

The tide was really low and I could see parts of the beach I don't remember ever seeing before. It felt very revealing, as if the beach was a woman who had hitched up her skirts, showing her sensual green swirling fronds and craggy rock pools to the passer by. I was struck by the vibrant sensuality of the beach, the swishing of the tides, the feel of sand crunching under feet, the wind tousling my hair. It was a sensual explosion as close to raw elemental nature as is possible living here in town. I let my feet move me and guide my path, ending up in a little cove further along than I had planned to go.

It was quiet and the silence seemed to swallow me up. Sitting in the growing dark it was like time stood still and I had been frozen along with it. I felt an affinity with the over exposed beach. It reflected the current state of my soul, being more exposed than it ever had before.

I have been stripped bare by the events of the last few weeks, stripped down to my essence of humanness and vulnerability. It is terrifying but also liberating. Here I am, just me, stripped of pretences and with the cupboards of my past flung open. I have bared my soul in a way I never thought I could do and survive, or rather, be able to do and still be able to function as a human. But I am more than just functioning now, that was what I had been doing. I had been holding my breath, hoping no-one would discover my secrets, and fearful of what would happen if I delved too deeply into my past. But here I am and All Is Well.

I sat so still in that little cove listening to the sounds of silence that a spider ran over my face, startling me. I got up and walked home.

Thursday 15th April

It is amazing how clean my house can be when I have a guest coming over. Leanne came for lunch and stayed the whole afternoon. I had spent the whole morning cleaning my house.

She is an interesting woman and I got to know her better today. I hope we will be friends. She has such a wealth of experience from so many births of all different types and varieties.

After only two experiences my vision is still so small, short sighted in some ways. For this reason, Leanne was keen for me to get out to more births without letting this last one colour my vision permanently.

'It would be easy for you to just to stop now, say it's not for you and do something else,' she said, over the allotment-inspired lunch on the table.

'But you must be aware that although your presence has an impact on the dynamics of any situation, you are not responsible for the outcome. Mama and Papa are the ones in charge. Your job is to be there for them, to help re-establish their rhythm if it gets interrupted but also to know when to step out again. Be their advocates when they are busy, protect their space and remember their wishes. But ultimately they are responsible for themselves and their birth.'

I let out a sigh as the final bits of that feeling released and I felt my shoulders drop down. I hadn't even been aware that they were tense until then.

We ate overlooking the sea, which was smooth and calm today. The afternoon passed in a blur as we sat drinking tea and talking about birth.

We spoke about the couple that I would be meeting later. Leanne told me of their attendance at her active birth classes and of their birth plan, which was for a very low-key home water birth. She had seen so many people go into labour with their birth plan and come out the other end with a totally different experience.

I wondered what was it that made it possible for some births to follow their pre-written plan and for others to go so far from it. Leanne identified a few factors that helped influence how birth might go. She made a point of saying that many things can affect labour once it has started and promised we would look at these later.

For starters, she said, birth preparation helps enormously and this is helpful on many levels. Labour and birth are physically demanding for both mother and birth partner so being in good shape physically helps a great deal. Many people these days are likening labour to running a marathon, though not necessarily true since marathon runners don't get the extreme flow of hormones that birthing mothers do. But it's a useful image for the challenge.

Being mentally prepared means getting life ready for the practicalities of birthing. The knowledge of the natural birth process is useful in understanding how to encourage a natural birth without need for medical intervention.

We talked about oxytocin, which has been dubbed the love hormone and its important role at birth. This is the hormone that is released when we fall in love, experience orgasm, give birth and breastfeed. It made sense that what put baby in the womb in the first place is what would help the mother in giving birth and sustaining her during the early months. Yet oxytocin is also a shy hormone, best released when the environment is private, dimly lit and feels safe and secure, like the environment we enjoy for making love.

Birthing is also something instinctive and comes from the part of our brain called the primal brain. The thing about evolution is that our thinking brain, or neo-cortex, has the capacity to overrun and shut down the primal brain. This could be triggered by asking the birthing woman lots of questions. If she has to think about things it brings her out of intuitive mode into rationalizing mode. Turning on all the lights and doing lots of examinations could also make that switch happen.

Outside the window, I could see the tide was beginning to shift now and flow out. Boats were turning around with the flow of water. It struck me how the tide was like birthing. Understanding how tides ebbed and flowed without trying to stop them or control them meant that things could flow easily. If the boat owners tried to keep their boats still and stop their boats from turning with the water as the tide turned, their boats would suffer damage in the process. By understanding the natural ebb and flow of the tide, the boats were allowed to move freely along with the swirling waters.

I wanted to find out more about what Leanne had hinted at in her email about our birth paving the way for our life.

'It is all to do with hormones,' she said. 'This isn't just some hippy midwife's intuition, this is scientific fact. But the research has been quite controversial especially when seen through the medical profession's tinted glasses. However it is accepted fact that there are critical periods in a human's lifetime when health and personality could be influenced.'

'Is our health influenced by our genes or by the environment?' I asked.

'Good question, the classic nature versus nurture debate,' she replied. 'It is a combination, and sometimes the environment can unlock something that is held within our genes. It is suggested that our adult health is determined while we are in the womb, which is why there is so much nutritional advice for pregnant woman. Links have been found between our life in the womb and illnesses like obesity, heart disease and diabetes in adult life. It is also suggested that our birth can affect our personality, especially our levels of aggression and capacity to love in adult life.'

I was shocked. 'Why have I never heard this before? And why would anyone want to interfere with the natural process of birth if it has such lifelong consequences?'

My mind was whirring, thinking of my own birth and what that might say about who I was. I was also thinking of Valentina, how she slid out into welcoming hands, opposed to how Anne-Marie's baby arrived. It felt almost cruel how he had been dragged from the birth canal. But I had thought that was just my own feelings. Here, Leanne was telling me that birth had a bigger impact on our whole lives.

'There is more.' She continued. 'Things like autism, criminal tendencies, drug addiction and anorexia have all been linked to childbirth. There is scientific research out there documenting this, it is just a question of looking in the right places. I can't say for sure why modern birth in the western world is so medical. I am not against caesareans or assisted birth. They have undoubtedly saved many lives in their time. But the sad fact is that like many technologies they have been abused as well. Scheduled caesareans planned to fit in with busy timetables and forceps delivery when the doctors get impatient waiting for the baby to descend. These are unnecessary interventions and that is the difference between saving lives and interfering with nature. It is difficult now as many midwives have lost the knowledge of the natural birth process, relying instead on machine readouts and drug dosage. Birth was once an art and now it is a science.'

'But isn't science a good thing?' I was getting confused.

'Science is a good thing, but too much knowledge without wisdom is not such a good thing. Every birth is different because every woman is different, though there are common factors. It is good to be aware of how we birth physiologically and psychologically, which is why in the training weekend we watched videos of women birthing naturally. In order to understand how birth works, we have to study the natural uninterrupted birth process. It is one thing to know something scientifically but it is another for that to become accepted by culture as a whole. It is a process that can take a long time to bear fruit and become accepted. When my first son was born it was routine for babies to be separated from their mothers in hospital. He was kept in a nursery down the hallway. I wasn't allowed to pick him up when I wanted to until they let me go home. Things have changed a lot since then. Things are changing every day. That is why our work as Doulas is so vitally important. This is not just a job.' She was becoming excited now. I could feel her passion for the subject rising. She wasn't in this for the money either.

'By being Doulas we are assisting not only these women to have the birth they want but also the next generation to begin their lives in the best way possible. Their birth is the launch pad of their whole lives. We want to be there to welcome them into the world with love. It is not just a job. It is a service to mankind. We are literally birthing the future.' She sat back on her chair, eyes ablaze, spirit on fire.

'Wow, that is incredible,' I replied. 'Absolutely incredible.'

'It sure is. Did you have any idea what you were getting yourself into when you signed onto the course?' she laughed. 'You know some people really get this, the whole future of humanity thing. Other people don't, it's just a job to them. But actually I feel it doesn't matter too much. As long as we are doing our job with love and respect, honouring the passage of birth as a natural process, we are doing what needs to be done. We may be the minority right now but there will come a time when we will create a tipping point and birth culture will change, then life on earth will change. It is an exciting time. We are living history.'

'From the moment I found out what a Doula was, I was enthralled,' I admitted to her. 'The whole idea sent shivers up my spine, like it was something bigger than who I am. Who I am doesn't seem so important seen from the bigger perspective.'

'Yes, it is bigger than just you. But don't be fooled, you are very important.' Her eyes turned serious now. 'Who you are is unique. You take your special gifts with you wherever you go. But you also bring your wounding. We talked a bit about it on the phone and during the training weekend. You have seen trauma in your life, most of us have. This last birth you attended triggered something deep within you, something that you need to work on healing: your own birth. Science says our birth affects us, so work with that. What do you have to learn? What do you have to let go of in order to move forward? Where are you going with this?' My mind went forward to this couple that was looking for a Doula. With what I now knew, could I be there for them to nurture their vision and assist their child into this world? Maybe that was it, maybe it was all about healing. It was time to heal. I felt ready to step forward, to accept what life had served me, this golden opportunity to serve mankind. I felt light headed but also very grounded and aware of the reality. There was a job to be done and I was the person to do it.

The afternoon was wearing on and my time with Leanne was coming to a close. I needed to focus on what was important for me to talk about with this couple later so that we were on the same page. It made it easier knowing that they had studied active birthing with Leanne and knew most of this. We weren't starting from ground zero.

It was quite late in this woman's pregnancy. The baby would be already fully physically formed in the womb. The final touches were being made. Like the transfer of temporary immunities from mum to baby to protect it during the first stage of life. Leanne reminded me that before doing anything, it is important to check in with myself about how I am feeling. Was there anything I needed to do before I could be present for someone else? Then check in with the couple and how they are feeling. It is important to listen to them before continuing and deal with any questions that come up.

I also had a list of questions to share with them. If there had been time, it would have been a good idea to send it to them beforehand to allow the couple to discuss them privately. Still, it was a start.

What kind of birth are they hoping for?
Why do they want a Doula?
What do they want their Doula to do?
What are their hopes and fears about a Doula?
What role does the father want to play?
What role does the mother want the father to play?
Current experience of pregnancy?
Previous experiences of pregnancy including abortions / miscarriages / other sexual trauma (*This may be appropriate to talk about or may be better for another meeting. We'll see how things go*)
Hopes and fears around birth?
Relationship with midwife/doctor/hospital?
Talk about having Leanne as a back-up Doula
Set up further meetings before birth.

Their projected due date is the tenth of May, which gives us four weeks to prepare. But remembering that only two per cent of babies come on their due date I would have to be on call for them for two weeks before that date. That is only two weeks away from today. Depending on how today goes and if we all agree to work together we could theoretically arrange two more meetings before being on call.

This approach felt more grounded. It was a healthy way to approach being a Doula for someone. I felt inspired from talking with Leanne, with a fire burning in my soul. After she left I sat to write these words before I forget them. In a little while I'll go and meet them. I am feeling so much more prepared this time.

Friday 16th April

Another journey has begun. The couple I met last night were called Anna and Roy. From the moment I went into their home I felt welcome.

They have one of those homes that don't look like anything extraordinary from the outside but as soon as you go in you realize that these are people who not only appreciate beauty but have the capacity to bring it into their home. It was airy and spacious, with simple line drawings of ballet dancers and women relaxing on the walls, a smell of fresh flowers filled the hall. Their living room had large comfy sofas in front of an open fireplace that just invited snuggling up and unwinding. We sat sipping fresh mint tea from the garden as we got to know each other.

Anna had been a dancer until they had decided to try for a baby. This pregnancy had come after two months off the pill.

She was the epitome of grace, the way she moved and the way she sat ~ even with her large rounded belly she had that air about her.

Roy worked at home in their converted attic with a view over the estuary. He was a website designer. 'Work is good,' he said. 'It provides a steady income and is also flexible enough that I can enjoy living.' They smiled at each other at he said this.

We got into the questions I had brought after I had checked in with them about how they were feeling. Anna shared how they had been enjoying the support of the classes. Hearing positive birth stories was empowering and had confirmed their choice of a home birth.

We began talking about why they felt they wanted a Doula and I found out it came as a recommendation not only from Leanne but also from their midwife, Sally. By coincidence it was the same midwife I knew. Since then they had done some research and read about how having a Doula can reduce the need for medical intervention and pain relief. They were hoping to have as natural a birth as possible.

Being a dancer, Anna had first-hand experience of how strong her body could be. She was full of conviction that birth was a totally natural and normal event in a woman's life. This had been confirmed during her antenatal check-ups as the pregnancy was progressing well with no problems. Baby was currently head down in the LOA position, which I remembered was the ideal place for first time mums and increased the possibility of an easy birth.

We talked about what they saw my role as, which was to be their support person. Roy was open with me about his fears about the birth, mainly about not knowing what was going on and feeling like he had to know everything.

They wanted me to be there if he needed a break, also to be able to have someone to commit to being with them throughout the whole labour, rather than having a change when someone's shift ended, felt important to them. That need for continuity was something I had heard that was wished for by other mothers. They said how frustrating it felt, that midwives might come and go during labour and that they might not even know the midwife that arrived. This way I would already know them, know their birth plan and be there in the moment to help them optimize the environment for that plan to happen. I would also be their advocate if that became necessary.

It felt like a good moment to bring up the issue of having Leanne as my back-up Doula in case I couldn't get there, despite the fact that I only lived down the road and she lived a couple of hours away. They were fine with this idea, especially as they already knew Leanne. It also took the pressure off me feeling I would be solely responsible.

They had been worried both about not finding a Doula in time and also of not getting along with them. I told them that they didn't need to make a decision right then. We would spend the first meeting talking then have some time to think about it before any of us committed to working together. After all I am still a trainee Doula with my mentor behind me. Maybe they would prefer someone fully trained.

I was honest about where I was in my training. It is part of my new found integrity of being true to myself and those around me. No more closed cupboards for me if I can possibly help it, I thought to myself.

They had planned a home water birth having heard about how great warm water was to encourage relaxation during labour. Anna loved hot baths and took one almost every day at the moment, using the time to listen to her relaxation CD. She told me about how the most important thing for her during this birth was that her baby be welcomed into this world softly and lovingly.

She felt that the transition from the watery womb to the air breathing world could be softened for the baby by first coming through water. Babies will not try to breathe until they feel the air and the umbilical cord will continue to pulse with blood from the placenta until it comes into contact with air. They had been given a birthing pool by some friends whose second labour had been so quick they didn't have time to even set it up!

This had given Anna and Roy another reason to have a Doula present, due to the extra work involved setting up and keeping the water in the pool at the right temperature. Roy didn't want to have to be constantly thinking about those logistics when he wanted to be by Anna's side during labour, preferably in the pool with her. So another one of my roles would be checking and maintaining the pool temperature, which for birthing is around thirty seven degrees Celsius. They had already had it out of its box and filled it up for a trial run in the front room. They found it comfortably fitted both of them and that there was plenty of space around it for the midwife and Doula as well.

They wanted to be able to concentrate on each other without having to answer the door to the midwife, make phone calls, keep water bottles filled up, and prepare snacks ~ other things that would be part of my role. Then we discussed post birth and what would happen. Something easy to forget in all the preparation for birth is that at the end of all this there would actually be a baby to take care of.

Again Anna talked about how birthing was a natural process from beginning to end and she saw no need to have drugs to expel the placenta unless really necessary. After she got out of the pool with baby there would be the cleaning up, emptying of the pool and settling in with new baby to organize. I would be there to help but also another friend had offered to come over after the birth to bring food and help tidy up. She didn't want to be there for the birth but wanted to help out in this way. Another time we would talk about postnatal visits, possibly two or three they said. First we had to decide if we wanted to work together.

We finished talking and I said my goodbyes to walk quietly home. My role seemed to be growing, but it felt like it was clear. From what we had discussed, my role would include helping them to understanding their hopes and wishes for the birth as stated in their birth plan as well as being their advocate if necessary. They wanted my continued presence and support throughout labour. I could also help them understand what was going on in the birth process. There were various ways I would be supporting Roy in his role as birth partner ~ by monitoring and maintaining pool temperature, cleaning and clearing up afterwards including emptying the pool. I would also be the receptionist, on door and phone patrol as well as welcoming the midwives. I would be their catering assistant by providing drinks and snacks

Then after the birth, I would be helping the new family settle in and possibly doing postnatal visits to help with breastfeeding and adjusting to life. It was a lot to think about. Just writing all that down made me realize just what a lot of different things are involved in having a home birth. It made me wonder just how Dads could manage to do all of that stuff on their own.

I feel like I would like the opportunity of working with them after our meeting yesterday. I will wait and see what they have to say. We discussed payment, and although I was happy to work for free at this stage Leanne told me it can be better to charge something, even if it's only to cover expenses. She has heard of Doulas not being contacted for the birth after weeks of meetings because labour started in the early hours and the parents decided at the last minute not to disturb the Doula. This could still happen of course but if someone feels like they have paid something for a service they are more likely to use it. I gave them a nominal fee to consider.

They have phoned and said they would be delighted if I would be their Doula. I said the feeling was mutual and we set up our next meeting for the coming week.

Saturday 17th April

After a full day up on the allotment, I came home in time to catch Ben ringing me on the phone.

My nails were caked in mud and it crunched as I picked up the phone. Hearing his voice made me feel surprisingly good. How could we not have been in contact for so long as we both sat within the walls of our beliefs? It's hard to believe. But I also realized that I have only told Angelica and Hilary that I have re-established contact with him. Talking about it with mother is not high on my priority list. How do I even begin to tell my brother?

My father was phoning to say hello since I had told him he could phone anytime. We spoke a bit about my recent experiences with the new couple.

He asked again about meeting up. He would be coming down to my neck of the woods in a week's time for a meeting with someone. He was wondering about having lunch together somewhere. I thought about it and found I was terrified for some inexplicable reason. I realized that if I didn't do this now then when would it happen? I agreed, opening myself to those feelings seeping through me.

It seems like my diary, which hadn't been used for appointments for a long time, is suddenly filling up. Life is waking up. Much as spring is bursting into life around me with trees in their summer greenery full of nesting birds, my own life is holding unexpected surprises.

Ben asked about my brother and I told him of his good boy act around my mother and his life as far as I knew of it. We have certainly drifted apart, not living in the same town, or holding to the same morals. I am not sure he ever really forgave me for leaving. His feeling is that it was his duty as son to stand by his mother and he felt I should also play the good girl act alongside him. We send Christmas and birthday cards but little besides, not having any common points of reference. I wondered how he would feel knowing that I was in contact with our father again. I could almost hear his voice in my head.

'He left us Joy, up and left and never sent a word to us in all this time. How could you even think of forgiving him after all that? He gave us nothing and I want nothing now.'

But that was just my imagination. Maybe he would be interested. I could write him a letter about it but

~ 152 ~

probably not until after I have met our father in the flesh.

The seedlings in the greenhouse are doing well, with their green lush leaves and strong straight stalks. It is amazing how well things can grow when you just give them the right environment with food, water, a dosage of love and encouragement. The pea plants need more support. They have broken out of being little seedlings and are finding their own way up to the light. I tied them gently to some small bamboo sticks until I can find something bigger to stop them trailing along the ground. The thing with pea shoots is that they are delicious, as every pigeon in the neighbourhood seems to be telling me these days. Sally has covered hers with netting and still they destroy her crop. I'm not sure how mine have managed to survive so far. I did make a scarecrow out of some old clothes back in February when there wasn't much to do up at the allotment and the dark days seemed to stretch forever. It doesn't look that realistic to me. Then again, I guess I'm not a pigeon!

Maybe I am a fool to forgive people for their mistakes. Yet I have also realized that our father is only a human and not some sort of godlike figure. We all have the capability to change. By forgiving him and not holding onto my hurt and anger, I forgive myself. The load I carry becomes lighter. I feel like a weight has lifted off my shoulders, making everything easier. Yesterday, and everything it holds, has gone. The people we were then have gone and we can only be present in today and what it brings. I think of some of the mistakes I made and how I have had to forgive myself and hope that others have been able to forgive me as well. I realize that by being forgiving, I don't feel weakened, in fact, quite the opposite. I feel empowered and brave. To be able to forgive and let go of the past, I feel more present and able to engage with what is going on now.

Angelica told me a story of how she had a boyfriend years ago who cheated on her while he was out on a stag weekend. She didn't know and he didn't tell her. Another friend told her and she confronted her boyfriend. She asked him why he had not told her what had happened. He said that he couldn't forgive himself for what he had done. He had not given her an opportunity to forgive him as he could not forgive himself. In the end he left her and later she met Nick.

I asked her how she had felt. Could she have forgiven what had happened? She replied that it had been horrible to find out from another person what had happened. If it had been from him it still would have hurt but that she had it in her to forgive.

'Forgiveness is what sets us free from the past and allows us to live in the present,' she said. As her boyfriend had not been able to let go, he had been stuck in that act and it had poisoned his present.

I have lived too long holding onto the pain of my youth with poison seeping into my bones and becoming part of who I was. I let that go now as I allow this new strength of forgiveness to sweep through me, washing out the bitterness from my heart.

Sunday 18th April

I spent today studying my notes from the Doula training course and preparing my assignments. There are also the required books on pregnancy and birth to be read and reviewed. Being aware that in a few weeks I am going to be at another birth brings my intention into focus.

How will it be? What will I do? Will it be like the last time?

I found a section on fear release in the manual and decided to work on my own fears about attending birth. It feels long ago now but it has actually only been four weeks since Anne-Marie gave birth and it still stings a bit when I remember. This technique talks about how a fear can be real or imaginary but that our brain cannot tell the difference and will react in the same way.

If a woman was birthing in a wood and saw an animal stalking her she would have no choice in how her body reacted. Adrenalin would be released into her system in the classic 'flight or fight' response. Adrenalin stops the flow of oxytocin, the love hormone. You cannot make love and be frightened at the same time. This adrenalin would probably stall or stop her body from birthing due to the threat posed to her baby and herself.

There may be no stalking animals in hospitals or homes but the imagined ones stalk the corridors of our minds.

'What if it hurts too much?'

'Will I lose control?'

'What if I embarrass myself?'

'They are all going to see my vagina and I feel ashamed.'

'I can't do it.'

~ 155 ~

'What if the baby is not healthy?'
'What if I die?'

My personal fears about being a Doula are more along to lines of: What if this birthing woman loses control and I don't know what to do? What if the birth has to move to hospital and becomes highly medical? What if I am not welcomed or scorned for my lack of knowledge and experience? What if I forget something or do something wrong? What if I make a total fool of myself?

I imagined that all of these things did happen. I imagined that I made a total fool of myself and did all the wrong things. I stood on the woman's hand and made her cry. Her husband called me nasty names. She couldn't birth at home and we had to go to hospital and they made me sit in the corridor. I let the fears run riot in my mind to their fullest and most horrible endings. I could never work as a Doula again. I was laughed out of town. I lost all my friends. My father was ashamed of me. I never could see another birth without crying. I sterilized myself to save myself from ever having to give birth.

I sat there and allowed my mind full rein in these crazy situations where my life had totally gone off the rails. Then, as I was at the most depressed bit of the story, as I had to undergo sterilization to avoid giving birth, I looked back and wondered just where I had started this nightmare of a fantasy?

I remembered it was when I had imagined standing on the birthing woman's hand and making her cry. Then it seemed somehow comical and a laugh escaped my mouth. I clapped my hand over it. I couldn't laugh at a birthing woman crying even if it was only in my imagination. Another laugh escaped around my hand and before I knew it I was howling with laughter at my own imagination.

How far had I gone in that crazy imagination from accidentally standing on a woman's hand to utter life devastation? I knew that it was all in my head. My imagination at its height was an incredible force and I realized I could use this tool.

When I had dried my eyes and drunk some water, I calmed down. I went back over this story of my worst fears. I saw myself standing on her hand and making her cry and instead of feeling shocked and stepping away, I acted with loving tenderness to her. I felt such a rush of love that the oxytocin level in the room doubled ~ since oxytocin levels are infectious and high levels in one person can set off a chain reaction of good feelings in others. This love rush, combined with her crying, meant that something shifted in her. She let go of some stress she didn't know she was holding and the birth went more easily as a result.

Then I imagined that her husband had called me nasty names. Instead of reacting, I didn't take them personally but let him vent his anger, rage and frustration until he began to calm down. Then he realized it wasn't me he was angry at but his own inability to stop feeling useless. I let him talk and express all his feelings, listening without judgement. In the end he found his inner peace and went on to be the most amazing dad.

I went back to the imagined scenario about being made to sit in the corridor at the hospital and used it as an opportunity to get to know the midwives and hospital procedure.

I could never work as a Doula again so I took up working in an orphanage.

I was laughed out of town so I joined a circus. I lost all my friends so became a nun. My father was ashamed of me so I had to give myself permission to forgive myself. I couldn't see births without crying so I bought shares in a tissue business. Instead of sterilization, I opted for abstinence.

I could beat my imagination at its own game, I realized. Either allow it to use me or use it as the tool that it was. I had heard of the mind being like a sharp sword, either learn how to wield it or be cut. And from this exercise, I came closer to understanding that today.

I remembered the story my grandpa told me about the three sillies. How the farm hand next door had come over to their farmhouse to ask for the daughter's hand in marriage. The daughter was sent into the cellar to pour some beer for her father, mother and suitor to drink in the kitchen. While pouring the beer, she saw a big hammer dangerously balanced above her. She imagined that she and the lad upstairs had gotten married. Then they had a daughter who one day had been sent into the cellar to pour some beer just like she was doing now. And just suppose, she thought to herself, that big hammer had fallen down and killed her little daughter! At this she started to cry and wail. Her mother came down to see what the matter was. When the daughter had told her mother what might happen she too began to weep and wail. The father came down to see what the matter was. When the daughter had told her father what might happen he too began to weep and wail. Eventually the lad came down. When he found out what these three were weeping and wailing about, he called them the biggest three sillies he had ever seen and promptly removed the big hammer before leaving.

Monday 19th April

The sea called me today. Before I knew what I was doing I was pulling on my boots and grabbing a flask and my camera. It was early, the sun hardly up but what had called me so quickly was the most incredible swirling mist around the beach. It was very atmospheric as I walked alone along the deserted beach.

I went to a place I knew there would be stones and closed my eyes, allowing my hands to be guided to choose the stones I would want. It was such a special experience that I thought I may still be dreaming. I knew I wasn't fully awake and didn't feel like I really woke up the whole time. The beach does that to me.

By midday my stomach was crying out for food. The flask had long been emptied and I went home. But not without some great pictures of the stones that had jumped into my hands. These weren't very big stones, more like pebbles really, surrounded by swirling sea mist. The day had cleared by the time I walked home and I felt I had visited somewhere far away.

I ate quietly then went over the river to visit a project that had started as one man's vision but quickly became something more. It was a place that had encouraged a sustainable future, community living and self-sufficiency. They ran courses for kids from the city to spend time out of doors as well as learning more about themselves. They also ran other courses like forest schooling and handicrafts.

Hilary had invited me to come to their open day and we travelled together by ferry across the river. It was a different kind of place, quiet yet humming with activity. I met some interesting people, lots of families with little children and older kids busy doing things around the place. I realized that I had hardly ever before seen children doing things like carving wood or sewing clothes.

There were impressive gardens and after speaking with their gardeners I knew that most of their seeds were old varieties that self-seeded and could be passed on. They had regular seed swaps throughout the year and I put myself down on the email list as a willing volunteer.

Grandpa always told me to save the seeds. He showed me how to choose the best ones to save for the coming year to avoid having to buy new stock every season. That, combined with knowing your neighbouring gardeners, helped to diversify while remaining self-sufficient.

I loved the worm farm at the community. The fertilizer that came out of it looked like it could have grown anything. It was so rich and fertile. They also grew medicinal herbs for a wide spectrum of ailments. Herbal lore is something I hadn't explored much beyond mint and chamomile. Hilary remembered some of them from when she was nursing. Their lush cottage garden grew herbs to help women bring on labour, to speed up contractions, to increase milk supply, to help with shock, to stop haemorrhaging, to calm and soothe as well as to reinvigorate. I bought one of their books and some packets of dried herbs to start making teas for myself to try.

Tuesday 20th April

Why am I afraid of listening to my heart? I feel afraid that if I trusted it and let my father in, it would hurt more this time around. My automatic response is to just close down, to shut the door and not let anyone in. It feels like that has been my default programming for years. I guess that is what my mother has always done. I never saw a scrap of emotion from her, apart from anger and hostility. Sometimes I wonder how she lives with herself. I guess it's the anger that keeps her going. I wonder what would happen if she just stopped for a minute and let something else in. Would her whole world come crashing down?

Maybe I am the one to answer that because right now I am rewiring my programming. Going against what I was trained to do in the face of strong emotion and fear of loss and it feels terrifying, wonderfully terrifying. I feel like a parachutist about to jump from a plane. A buzz of adrenalin combined with the calm quiet interior as the inner critic is terrified into silence in the face of the prospect that awaits. And as I am falling out of the plane I realize that I don't remember packing my parachute. Did I do it? Am I even wearing one? My instinct for self-preservation sits up and begins to howl in the face of death. Yet still I feel calm as I watch scenes of my life rush past. My childhood spent in hand-me-down shorts and t-shirts. Knees scratched from climbing trees and fingernails full of dirt. Grandpa's shed and the sanctuary it was for me, filled with bowls of illicit pumpkin soup.

I see my adolescence whizz past in a blur, the days seeming to speed up with schoolwork and exams. I see myself packing my bags and leaving home. Then there was the long trip south to find a new life and wake up to the sea every day. Collecting shells with little holes in them and making mobiles. I see the lost loves of my life float past like ghosts. The men I have loved and left.

And now I remember what brought me into this reverie. The fact is that my father has come back into my life and is creeping into my heart. I become acutely aware of how this feels. There is blood beating in my chest. The sensation that life is changing and that some of my fundamental programs are in the process of being rewritten.

I am lying in bed and put my hand over my heart to feel it pumping. I feel my chest rising and falling with every breath. I think about all the information that comes into my body every time I breathe in. I can almost taste the soup of gases that make up air: water vapour, scent molecules, pollen, dust and plant spores. I look at the dust on my bedside table, reminding me it's time to do some housework, and wonder how much of that I breathe in again. That dust which is made up of my own dead skin cells, coming into my body again. Does that make me sneeze knowing it's something I have already discarded?

I didn't discard my father. I had no choice. And I don't think he meant to discard me or my brother. He suffered from shock and that put him into a place he didn't know how to get out of. There was nobody there to help him.

He sounded genuinely remorseful on the phone. It just feels like I still have a lot of anger in me towards him. It probably isn't even my anger but something I have learnt from growing up in the same house as my mother.

I had never really considered the fact that my grandma died giving birth to my mother and how that might have affected her. I can't begin to imagine what it was like. But maybe that has something to do with the amount of repressed feelings she has carried around all her life. As Leanne said, how we are born can affect our life.

Grandpa said he could never understand my mother's rage. Even when she was small she was angry. He was a sweet man and I always found it strange that she could have been his daughter. It was as if the sadness of losing her own mother the very day she was born twisted back into herself and became anger. This anger lashed out at everything close to her. When I was young that was me. I was the closest thing to her.

My brother knew how to stay out of the way. I just couldn't seem to hide. My flame red hair might have had something to do with it. I could never seem to keep it under control and it certainly wasn't anything like the thin, mousy brown hair she had. I was an explosion of redness and curls, untameable by brush or comb. Even hairbands and clips seemed to have a way of letting bits of it escape until there were strands flying everywhere.

Once when I was five years old, she had it all cut off to a short bob after I got some chewing gum stuck in the back. Grandpa said it was a shame. It didn't need that much cut off. He said that she did it because my red hair reminded her of my father. I wonder if he really does have wild red hair like mine. No one else in my family does. The Facebook photo only showed his face, not his hair.

Wednesday 21st April

I went back to the breastfeeding support group yesterday. There were familiar faces from last week's session and lots of them remembered my name which felt very welcoming. I am terrible at remembering names and I don't have to get up every night to breastfeed a small baby. But names never were my strong point; faces I will remember for years but not names. It is the same with streets. I can give you directions based on what places look like but don't ask what any of the streets are called.

I am glad I went back yesterday. Lots of the women were interested in talking about Doulas and what they do. Last week I had learnt a lot about breastfeeding and was more than happy to talk about Doulas. But as I spoke I realized that some of these women didn't need a Doula as they had close family support systems around them. One woman's mum came over almost every day to play with her toddler and take the baby out for a walk in the park. Another woman's mum had been at her birth and poured hot water over her back for hours. But not all the women were lucky enough to have families close by. Some had good friends and all of them drew strength from the weekly support group, as well as other places they went to meet with other mums.

Then a woman arrived with a tiny baby who was only five days old and I was able to witness the peer supporters in action. The mother was obviously extremely upset. Big black circles underlined the swollen red eyes that looked like they might spill with tears again at any minute. Her health visitor came in to introduce her to the trained volunteers as having multiple breastfeeding issues. She said that if the baby wasn't feeding effectively by the end of the day then they would be going into hospital. What an ultimatum!

The woman sank into a chair and was given a cup of tea while her baby was crooned over by the other mums. She looked like she had not had a chance to recover from the birth. As the story came out it became obvious that she was suffering from exhaustion and shock.

The labour had been long and slow, lasting a few days. After the birth she had not been able to get her baby to latch onto the breast correctly and neither had any of the health workers and midwives who poured through her home. They had suggested that she came to this group as a final attempt at breastfeeding before going to hospital, which probably meant going onto formula milk.

I didn't want to intrude on this woman's privacy. She was obviously having a difficult time but I didn't want to leave just yet. So I sat quietly as the other mums chatted away. I watched and listened to how the peer supporter volunteers handled her distressing situation. I was fascinated. They did it so well that at first I thought they must know her. They were kind and welcoming like she was an old friend. When someone asked her name, I realized with a jump that they had never met her before. It was touching how she was being treated with the sort of sympathy and concern normally reserved for good friends.

They listened to her talk about trying to feed around the clock. About baby coming off the breast crying, her sore nipples and her lack of sleep for days now. We heard about her arguing with her husband about what to do. Her mother-in-law had been telling her to just give him a bottle. Her breasts were aching, full with milk, and she felt useless not being able to feed her baby. Now with all this worry about having to go to hospital, she felt like the baby was not satisfied with her. The woes went on and on.

All the while, no one was telling her what to do or what she was doing wrong. Everyone was listening to her now. Some of the mums were nodding their heads, others were tipping theirs to listen better. It seemed that this woman told a story to each of them. That tired and exhausted part of them that was woken up throughout the night, that part that wasn't heard or respected. She spoke from her heart and the outpouring touched me deeply.

All this time her baby was quiet. His eyes were open. He seemed to also be listening. When she was done and had wiped her tears away, my eyes were damp.

Then baby started making a noise; it was now his turn. But this wasn't like the snuffling grunts the other babies I had heard here make when they wanted to feed. This was a high pitched siren of a cry. His mum burst into tears again and started undoing her top to get out her breast, but one of the volunteers stopped her.

'Let's hear what he has to say,' a volunteer said.

The mum stopped what she was doing and looked at her. But the volunteer was already looking at the baby, who was being held by another volunteer at that moment.

This baby had lungs and he could use them. His siren went higher and louder. We all watched and listened to him. Then he stopped, just like that. I swear he looked around the room, saw we were all watching and then started up again with his high pitched wail.

'Yes we can hear you,' the volunteer murmured to him while the woman holding him held him tighter and paced up and down the room a bit, rocking him gently.

'We can hear you,' she repeated.

He stopped again, looked around again. He saw his mum and looked at her.

'I can hear you, darling,' she said weakly. He yelled again but this time it was like someone had found the volume control button and the siren got quieter and the pitch lowered.

The volunteer passed him back to his mother, whose eyes were streaming with tears from having to hear her baby cry. But he had calmed down and was just sort of snuffling now. The volunteers brought cushions and helped the mum get comfortable before bringing baby to her breast. They gave her a few tips to encourage correct positioning and latch. Then they were breastfeeding.

The mother looked up almost in disbelief.

'It doesn't hurt!' she said.

We watched her baby gulping. There was no question about effective milk transfer now. This was a happily feeding baby.

The health visitor came in later and was very pleased. She said they could go home and she would check in with them tomorrow. The woman stayed for the rest of the session and made new friends with other mums, promising to come back next week.

I could hardly believe the change in this woman from the red rimmed, exhausted heap that had dragged herself in through the door to the smiling woman making friends and chatting.

After all the mums left. I had to ask these peer support volunteers their secret. How did they do that? They all looked at each other and laughed.

'We didn't do it,' they said. 'We just help them to do it themselves. Babies know how to breastfeed as part of the innate reflexes they're born with. We just help the mums to get comfortable so they can listen to what their baby is trying to tell them. Most people just need some help with positioning and attachment. These two today both really needed to be listened to. Occasionally it is something more serious, but not today.'

It seemed to them that ever since this baby had been born, everyone had been telling the mother what to do, what to think, and how she must feel. Nobody had really listened to how she felt. She had begun to doubt herself.

The baby also needed to have a good shout. Every time he had tried to express himself, his mum had misread it as a need to be fed. Then she thought that when he rejected her breast, he was rejecting her, so had doubted herself more and more and so the cycle went on.

Hopefully that support session had broken the negative cycle of miscommunication by bringing mother and baby closer into harmony with each other.

After seeing that yesterday, I went over to talk to Angelica today. I asked if it made sense to her, about babies knowing how to breastfeed and mothers just needing to be relaxed enough to understand them. She laughed and passed Valentina over to me.

'So?' I asked the little breastfeeding princess. She seemed to roll her eyes as if to say, 'Finally you are beginning to understand the wisdom of babies.' I laughed out loud.

We remembered those early days when Angelica stayed in bed all the time with Valentina tucked up next to her. How their lives flowed together quietly and calmly after the adjustment. She thanked me again for my support in those days. She also remembered how her mum had come and helped cook and clean. Angelica hadn't left the bedroom for days.

Could these simple things have been what made the difference? My eyes widening in understanding, I realized even more what a blessing having a Doula could be, especially in the early days.

This was the relaxed alternative, instead of rushing back into everyday household life. With someone else around to help with the day-to-day running of things, the new mother could have time to get to know her baby intimately.

Learning how their baby communicated to express their needs and emotions was like learning a new language and took lots of time and attention.

I had heard how the early weeks establish the supply of breast milk, which is why demand feeding is so important at the beginning. But it is also very physically and emotionally demanding ~ especially if you are not only trying to establish supply and demand but juggle daily life as well. Angelica had stopped everything and flopped into bed with her baby. Even then, she'd had her doubts and worries in the beginning. But could every mum and baby flourish given the right circumstances?

Thursday 22nd April

Slugs came out in force after last night's rain, to feast themselves on my allotment. The new seedlings needed pricking out in the greenhouse. Some are ready to be hardened off, to get ready for a life outside. I feel like that sometimes, I need to step out of my internal work before coming back to everyday living. It is challenging dealing with age-old programmes that no longer serve me. I have emotional baggage that has become too heavy to carry and is weighing me down.

Reconnecting with my father is both exhilarating and heavy at the same time. I am happy we are in contact but it also brings up so many old wounds to be healed.

The allotment saves me from being too stuck in my head. It brings me back to the physical reality of weeds and slugs. Even with their slimy presence, things are beginning to bloom.

The apple trees look promising this year. I sprayed them against scab before the blossom came in and they seemed to have really liked it. The peas were sprawling and ready for the big hazel sticks I finally found to fully support them on their way. Sally has the hazel trees on her allotment for coppicing. She shared some sticks with me in exchange for some herbs that I had dug up and separated. Mint and chives like to be rehoused every now and then so they were very happy to be sent off to a new home. It is funny how these plants feel almost like family. I talk to them enough, more than my mother at any rate, so maybe they are. Grandpa was right ~ plants love chatter.

Tonight I am meeting with Anna and Roy again. This time it feels different as we have committed to work together. On Leanne's advice, I made up a simple contract. It is a place to write down what my role is and how I am expected to work with them. A bit like getting a minimal payment, a written contract is more formal but mainly its purpose is to make things clear. For example, I am happy to come for postnatal visits, to hold the baby and do light housework, but I am not going to clean any floors. This way everything is clear, it has all been said and discussed well in advance.

I don't want a repeat of the last experience. Tonight I plan to talk about what will be my role in the event of a transfer to hospital or emergency situation. Feels like a good idea to have the discussion beforehand, just in case.

Also, tonight, I want to talk about birth culture, what environment they were born into, how they grew up, and what they believe. It is time to be straight and open and honest with each other about who we are, where we come from and where we are going. It feels challenging for me to be so direct but the need to know is strong.

There are also some relaxation exercises that are helpful. Though I know they have been practising with Leanne, it will be good for us to practice together.

Anna is thirty seven weeks pregnant now so the birthing time is coming. There is still time for us to work through some things and most importantly to build up rapport and trust between us.

I am feeling positive and supported in this experience, which makes me a stronger source of support for others.

Friday 23rd April

The meeting last night went well, although unexpected things were discussed. I held the space as Anna shared very personal information about some sexual trauma that had happened to her when she was a teenager.

We were talking about birth culture and somehow it just came up and bubbled over. I could see Roy knew about it, too. He tenderly held her hand while tears ran down her cheeks as she retold her story. I felt like the level of trust and intimacy in the room rocketed as she shared the most intimate of memories with me. She had been forced to have sex on a date and had gotten pregnant as a result. Her parents had been angry, outraged at her as though it were her fault. She consented to an abortion at their insistence.

My eyes were full of tears as she spoke about the feeling of loss she felt when she woke up in the hospital after the abortion. Only then did she realize that there had been a life growing in her. Its absence was felt more than its presence had been.

The doctor had talked harshly to her, saying that abortions can make further chances of conception more difficult and she should be more careful in future.

The pain had gently eased over the years. She had the chance to spend time with one of her closest friends during her birthing experience and in the early days of motherhood. This had been healing for Anna. Her eyes lit up when she spoke of that tiny baby and seeing the love that was born alongside it.

I felt that, although much of this trauma had been released, there might still be some held in her heart. I led a little ceremony to say goodbye to the baby that had taken root in Anna's womb all those years ago. It was a bit like a funeral. She said all the things she would have said if that baby were here. She talked about how she was sorry it couldn't have been born, but that she couldn't have looked after it as she was so young herself.

Roy was also in tears when he said how sorry he was that this had happened to Anna and the baby. He hoped the baby would rest in peace. I spoke of forgiveness: to the doctor who didn't know how hard his words had hit and to her parents, whose reaction was their way of dealing with the shock of becoming grandparents so early. Finally I spoke of forgiveness to the man who had done this. I don't know where the words came from but I just knew that they needed to be said.

The room was quiet, just the sound of tears being wiped and the sound of my voice dropping into the hole of grief we had opened.

I prayed that this man had found peace and had realized the consequences of his actions. I asked for Anna and Roy to see into their hearts, to see if they could forgive him for what he had done so that the past could lie quietly and not interfere with the present.

They nodded their heads and we sat silently while watching the candle's flame burning.

Later the mood changed and it felt as if something had lifted. We looked at each other through different eyes, having shared something deep and personal. I left after giving them both big hugs, feeling more connected and positive about our journey together. We hadn't really gotten into much more of the birth culture. I left them some homework to find out about their own births, think about how they had been raised and investigate what popular culture told them about birth.

Today I walked along the coast path for miles and miles, looking out to sea at the distant horizon. I could see so far, having a different perspective and new outlook. It was entirely different from being down on the beach where every wave that came crashing in looked bigger than the last one.

Saturday 24th April

Today was the day I met my father for the first time. We had arranged to meet in a café down by the harbour, the one that overlooks the boats coming in and going out. I sat at a table by the window, feeling nervous and fiddling with my zip as I scanned every face that came through the door. I knew it was him before I saw his face. The wild red hair that couldn't be tamed framed a familiar yet unknown face. I stood up as he walked towards me. I could see the tears falling down his face just before my own eyes misted up. He walked up to me and for what seemed like an infinite time, we just looked at each other.

'Joy,' he said.

'Ben,' I answered.

He reached out to pull me into a hug that had been a lifetime in the waiting. He was tall and broad. The wiry hair tickled my nose. He smelt like toast and pine trees. His shoulder had a dark patch from the tears running down my cheeks. Eventually we sat down and ordered coffee.

'So here you are, my little girl,' he started. 'I am so sorry. I was such a fool. How could I have walked away from such a beautiful girl?' He shook his head as if he couldn't believe it.

I couldn't stop looking at him. His face was so familiar, like something you know that you know but cannot place. I guess it was because he looked a lot like what I see when I look in a mirror. I have never seen anyone with such crazy hair. It was wiry, long around his shoulders, and the exact colour of mine. He reached over and stroked my hair as if he could read my mind.

'No question that you are my daughter then,' he smiled.

What do you say to someone that you have been having imaginary conversations with your whole life? Someone you have gone through the whole range of emotions with, from anger to hatred to apathy to longing to love. There were so many questions that they just seemed to get tangled and tripped up on my tongue before any of them could escape my mouth. I sat and looked at him as I sipped my coffee.

Finally I said, 'I have so much I want to talk to you about, so many questions, and so many things I want to know that I just don't know where to start.'

He laughed a bit nervously, 'We have got lots of time, my girl. We can take it nice and slow.'

So we did.

We sat and drank our coffee, watching the fishing boats coming in with the morning's catch. Then we walked along the promenade as the tide was going out. We walked along the sandy beach. Sometimes talking, sometimes just walking together in comfortable silence and stealing glances at each other. At lunchtime I took him to a restaurant with a view out over the bay and as we ate we talked more about our lives.

I heard about his love of writing. I heard about how he had never married again and after having a couple of girlfriends who were only attracted to him for his wealth, he had remained a bachelor.

He had an apartment overlooking the river and invited me to come and stay in the spare bedroom when I felt ready. I left the invitation open, still not sure about how I was feeling as the floodgates were opening to a lifetime of bottled emotion.

He was very interested in my work as an artist and after lunch I took him to the gallery. It felt a bit odd bringing him into my world. But it was great sharing my work with someone who appreciates it so much.

We talked about inspiration and how my work has been evolving lately from seascapes to anthropomorphic rock balancing. This took us to talking about birth work and my journey as a Doula. I realized that I wanted to hear my birth story from him again. It was different this time, being face to face.

We went to the park and sat on a bench. It was quiet with only a few people strolling around. I wanted to understand what it was that had shocked him so much as to make him stumble out of the hospital and never come back. He left his whole life that day and I needed to know more about why.

He told me again, as he had told me on the phone, how labour hadn't gone well. My mother had been drugged and the doctor had used instruments to drag me out. But still I couldn't understand how that had caused such a terrifying impact on him. Why had he left?

As he spoke, I realized what a gentle man he was. His life had been a quiet one. My mother was the dominant force in the home. Seeing her drugged and almost dead, the blood and trauma of my birth had made him lose touch with reality.

He confessed that long ago in his youth he had suffered from mental health problems but he had thought they were behind him.

The birth had triggered something and it was like a connection in his brain had fired. He left the hospital and didn't know who he was. He had gotten lost on the city streets and stumbled around for a long time until he was found and cleaned up by that charitable organisation. By then all hope had left him. He was a shell of the man he had been, full of remorse and guilt.

I questioned him about his own family. Where were his parents? Where were my grandparents? The answer was like a stone in his mouth. They had died when he was younger. He had no brothers or sisters, no direct family.

'No distractions,' he said sadly.

Which explained how had been able to throw himself into software programming, working long hours every day of the week. More questions bubbled up but there was not enough time today to answer them all. He had to leave for his meeting.

We said our goodbyes and promised to stay in touch. More tears fell as we hugged goodbye. How could this have taken so long to happen? All those lost years stretched out like a line of empty plates that longed for a slice of love or caring. But today my plate had been filled.

I felt full of feelings. I felt love and sadness almost in equal measure as he walked away. So happy to have found this man who was my father and so sad to see him walk away again. But this time I knew it would be different, there was to be a tomorrow and he would be a part of it.

Sunday 25th April

Angelica and Nick came over with Valentina this morning. We went out for a walk through the woods together to see the bluebells in their resplendent glory. Later we went to have lunch at a country pub. We sat in the warm sunshine eating roast dinner.

It was a day of eating and digesting. I am appreciating my friends. They listened as I told them my story of meeting my father, asked questions and heard my story as it unfolded. They have been with me through so much these past weeks. Dragged me out of gloom and despair and rejoiced with me in times of elation and happiness. I couldn't ask for more from them. They are like the family I never had.

They both come from regular families and their parents are still together. Life has gone on pretty much the same since they were small. But they still have their own issues.

Nick spoke about how authoritarian his father was with him when he was growing up. Emotions and feelings were simply not discussed in the family home. His mum would just bow down to whatever decision his father made. Nick had been disciplined by being criticized, blamed and yelled at. He had been threatened and, on occasion, whacked for misbehaviour. The atmosphere at home had been always tense and so rigid it was oppressive. There was no discussion and only blind obedience to authority had been expected, nothing else was tolerated. As a child, Nick had felt scared and powerless. He now thought that his father had hidden behind this front of ruling without question, as it was what he had learned from his father, an old army captain. Nick had been a disappointment to his parents when he told them he was going to go to college to study photography. They had hoped for a more academic or military career for their only son. His sister was a career woman and he could never live up to the standard she had set. Still he had found his happiness in life, and it didn't come from being wealthy or a high achiever. He gazed at his partner as she held their daughter and sighed.

'This is real wealth,' Nick said. 'It's more precious than any jewel.'

Angelica rested her hand on one of his cheeks and kissed him tenderly on the nose. It is touching to see two people so much in love.

I had never known about Nick's family background. It amazed me how much he had managed to break out of that mould and follow the path of his own heart. Our families are such an integral part of us. Even if we don't believe we have been influenced by them, we have received their imprint during our early childhood. How much of the way we see the world and our place in it comes from what we have been taught to believe by our parents?

Nick's parents had run out of power over him when he stood up to them and walked away from their expectations. He had realized that the threats and criticisms were not something he had to listen to anymore. After that his life had changed overnight. He still kept in touch with them and spoke with them on the phone. But there remains an unresolved emotional distance between them, as they didn't have the tools to communicate their emotional needs.

I thought about my own upbringing with my mother. Sometimes she was violent and threatened to hit me when I was naughty. But mainly she was just mean. She would say horrible things and humiliate me in front of other people. She would tell lies about what I had done to gain more attention for herself.

As soon as I was old enough, I spent most of my time out of the house ~ at school, in clubs or with Grandpa up at the allotment. He never criticized or was mean to me. He was encouraging and seemed to love me unconditionally. He listened to everything I said, often while bent over weeding his plot or picking through the earth, clearing out stones. Any problems I had were mulled over thoughtfully.

Then he would look up and ask, 'What do you think would sort this out?' Raising an eyebrow at me as if it was obvious and I knew what the answer was.

Then I would somehow know what to do. The answer would pop into my head and I would throw my arms around his neck and kiss his whiskery cheek.

'Thanks, Gramps, you're the best,' I would proclaim.

'I didn't do nuffin' my love, you're the brains around here,' he would chuckle in reply.

When I was with him I felt happy, secure and loved. I couldn't do anything wrong, although I did make mistakes sometimes which I then had to help sort out. Like the time I put weed killer instead of plant food into the watering supply and all his greenhouse plants died overnight. He was so sad and sat down with his head in his hands. I felt terrible even though it had been an honest accident.

I remember he looked up and said to me, 'So what'll we do then, lass? How will we get this lot going again?'

I decided I would go around the allotment and tell everyone what I had done and ask for any extra plants they might have.

He looked at me and asked if I really wanted to do that and I said I did so we went around together. By the end of the weekend his greenhouse was fuller than ever with a whole new selection of plants, many of which he hadn't had before. He was very happy that my solution had been a good one, even though it had been hard telling everyone about my mistake.

Monday 26th April

Tonight I went to the local home birth support group which meets bi-monthly in a neighbouring town. I was surprised to hear that one even existed when Sally mentioned it last week. I had dropped over to her allotment to swap seedlings. She told me the group was run by volunteers, mainly antenatal teachers and other birth workers. There was usually a midwife present as well.

Sally told me why she enjoyed being at a home birth. Not only because her work was reduced, as the birthing couple were often more prepared, but also that she was able to devote herself to being with just one family instead of trying to monitor various women in different rooms up and down the corridor, as could happen in hospital.

I asked her about the local home birth rate and she said it was quite high. This was probably due to the support available locally, in the form of the support group as well as a team of local midwives who were happy to attend at home births.

The group met this evening and I went along to see what was going on. Anna and Roy had told me that they had been a couple of times before and invited me to join them tonight.

It was informal and relaxed, located in a village hall. Sally often came but was on a call tonight. I was struck by the work of the volunteers who run the group, believing so passionately in what they are supporting that they do it even though they aren't being paid. It occurred to me that perhaps I could become a volunteer as well one day.

But this evening was about finding out what support was available and having the opportunity to talk to other people who'd had home births. People who were planning home births and professionals who were there to give advice could all be sources of information for me.

There was another Doula there who also worked locally, but was located north of my town so our paths had not crossed before. She hadn't trained with Leanne but with someone else in the city whose approach was quite different. I could see we were going to have a lot to discuss and we swapped numbers to stay in touch.

There were quite a few dads-to-be there, all standing in the corner around a birth pool. They were discussing various methods for filling and emptying it.

Some pregnant women were moving around with their beautiful big bellies. Their birthing time isn't far away I realized. All were interested in hearing home birth stories. They were normally the minority and this group was a chance for them to be with like-minded people. For them, birth was a normal, natural event and hospitals should be reserved for emergencies only. They didn't think what they were doing was in any way extreme or dangerous or that they were trying to prove something. It was just that home was where they felt the most comfortable and relaxed.

Someone pointed out that the best environment in which to birth a baby would be similar to the environment needed to conceive. This led onto the talk by the midwife in attendance about love hormones. She explained how the same hormones for breastfeeding and birth were present during love making and falling in love. All of these acts of love were like pictures on a story board, in my mind, all natural progressions of each other which had to be followed in order. Breastfeeding followed birthing which followed making love which followed falling in love. They also all included that shy hormone, oxytocin.

The midwife talked about birthing being a natural process that could be easily disturbed by questioning and bright lights. It was something I had heard before and I suspected many other people present had as well. It helped to confirm that what these couples were planning to do was natural and normal. I could see heads nodding around the room as she spoke.

'Home birth was once the norm,' she said. 'Birthing only moved to the hospital when male doctors began to get involved in the delivery of babies. At first there were many women who died in hospitals due to poor sanitary conditions. It is much easier to keep a house clean than a whole hospital where many germs come to breed.'

'Hospitals can be good places with facilities that undoubtedly save lives and restore the balance of health,' she continued. 'And some women feel more secure and comfortable birthing in a hospital knowing that if they needed assistance then they wouldn't have to transfer to one. It is all about listening to your own feelings and going with what feels best to you.'

Her message was not biased either way. It was about feeling safe inside yourself to allow those hormones to flow.

I liked her. She was open, honest and forthcoming. She knew her subject, having been a local midwife for many years. She wasn't trying to tell people that home birth was best, rather that it was a viable and safe option to give birth. I could see that she was trying to normalise home birth, and make it accessible. But in a way she was preaching to the converted here at this group. Most of them, if not all, had already set their hearts on having a home birth. Regardless, she gave useful information and it was empowering for the couples assembled to know that they had someone in the health profession who was on their side and understood their decision to birth at home.

Later, Anna and Roy chatted with another couple that had given birth at home two months ago. They had brought their baby along to the group to share their story. I was listening in to their conversation when I saw someone I recognized across the room.

I went over and said hello to the volunteer I had met the previous week at the breastfeeding support group. She was six months pregnant and had come with her husband as they were considering having a home birth. They already had a toddler who had been born in hospital by emergency caesarean section and she didn't want to repeat the experience.

They had enjoyed listening to the midwife talk as a lot of what she had said had been quite new for them. Well, probably newer for the husband. I got the impression that she had done quite a bit of reading and had persuaded him to come along to the meeting to meet other people who also believed that home birth was natural and safe.

He was looking a little nervous about the whole idea so I took him over to meet Roy, who, by now, had left Anna and the other woman to talk and was chatting with the other dad. I introduced them and briefly outlined the situation before leaving them to talk. I took the peer supporter over to meet Anna, who was holding the baby and talking about breastfeeding. Great timing!

I left them, too, and went to catch the midwife before she left. I wanted to introduce myself and make her acquaintance. Her name was Gloria. She was not easily missed in her large flowery dress and wide- mouthed smile. She looked like someone who could sweep you up and protect you from the world at large. I knew she must have made a lot of birthing women feel very safe by her presence alone. She welcomed me warmly to the group, having seen how having a Doula can help not only the birthing family but also her, as the midwife.

'Sometimes my shift ends and I have to hand over to the next midwife during the middle of labour,' she explained. 'When there is a Doula with the family who I know will be there right until the end, I don't feel so bad leaving. This continuity of care is a real issue for us. Doulas help to bridge that gap. They are also cheaper than drugs,' she laughed.

I hadn't even thought about the price of drugs being on people's minds when they were thinking of hiring a Doula. But maybe it was the hospital's perspective. She had heard of Leanne and some of her clients had taken antenatal classes with her.

I complimented Gloria on her talk, I had really enjoyed it and found it resonated with the way that I worked and saw birth. I am glad I made the effort to connect with her. She could be the midwife at a birth I attend. I want her to know that I am an ally.

Anna and Fern (the pregnant peer supporter whose name I finally remembered) and the other mum had really hit it off. When I went back they were exchanging phone numbers and arranging to meet up. Things wound down. We said our goodbyes and left.

I caught a lift home with Anna and Roy. They were glad that I had come and seen the place where they were drawing their support. It was just another thing that put us on the same page in regards to birth preparation.

But when they were joking about looking at women's bottoms in the pool while watching birthing videos, I felt a pang of something that worried me. I couldn't join in their laughter and just looked out of the window not knowing what to say.

Maybe there were other things we needed to share. How comfortable were they being naked in front of each other and with their bodily functions? Had they ever had to vomit while the other one held their hair? Or seen each other in less than perfect physical conditions? That could affect things I thought to myself and made a mental note.

I told them I would see them on Thursday for another meeting at their house to talk about birth culture. As I said it, I realized that I, too, need to do some preparation for that meeting.

I have been doing a lot of digging around in my own personal past. How I was born and raised and how that feels to me now. But how do I feel about current popular culture? How do I fit into what is happening here in the modern western world? Am I making informed decisions based on scientific fact or am I going with my gut feeling? Or is it a mixture of both? How much of what I believe has been fed to me by the media? How much is programmed by my upbringing? How much is cultural or personal? How comfortable am I around nakedness and bodily functions? There are lots of things to consider.

When I got home and looked at the calendar, I realized that I am officially on call for Anna's birth from today. Her estimated due date is only two weeks away but the baby could come any time now. It feels like we still have some preparation to do and I am feeling the pressure of time running out.

Tuesday 27th April

This morning I bought a pile of baby magazines from the local newsagents. On the covers were lots of glossy photos of beautiful, clean, smiling babies and perfectly beautiful mums in full make up, looking slim and bubbling with happiness. I found a magazine that showed how photos of celebrity mothers' bellies had been digitally adjusted to make them look slimmer for their post-birth photos. It must be such a compelling image for a new mum, these women in the magazines with perfectly tucked tummies.

It's hard to know what is real these days since many images of women in the press and adverts have been so altered digitally that they no longer look like real people.

Where are the stretch marks, the black bags from lack of sleep and the soft tummies from carrying babies for nine months? Where are the laughter lines and grey hairs of wisdom and experience? They have all been airbrushed out to be replaced by these unreal beings with perfect skin, hair and nails. Most of the magazines were adverts for baby items, such as cots and clothes, pillows and blankets, nappies, skin care products and toys, bras and breast pads, laundry soap, cleaning wipes, sun cream and oils, books, CDs, slings and pushchairs that looked like space stations, with climate control and drink holders.

I felt overwhelmed by the amount of cute and tantalizing things I could buy. Is this my culture, consumerism and wealth? I guess it is for some people.

To make it easier to see, I started to cut out images and pasted them onto a big sheet of paper, making a kind of collage of images from each magazine. I couldn't find any other kind of magazines at the newsagents so I looked online. There I found such a wealth of images and information that it was overwhelming. I needed to find an entry point, someone to point me in the right direction. Just googling 'baby' was inconceivably vast, with 3,000,000,000 results!

I emailed the group of women I had studied with on the Doula course. Some of them wrote straight back with wonderful links to websites they liked. I spent the rest of the day surfing the internet, finding groups all over the world who believe childbirth to be a normal event in a woman's life. These groups felt that many items for sale were unnecessary. The basic needs of a baby are warmth, love and breast milk.

I realized that the birth culture that most resonated with me was not defined to one country or one religion but spanned the globe. I found American, Australian, South African, South American, Hawaiian, and European groups and teachers all over the world that held the same message. There was research that backed up some things that women felt instinctively, such as how holding a new-born increased milk supply and reduced stress in mother and baby. It was this research that changed the hospital procedure of routinely separating mothers from their new-borns.

I really felt like a global citizen today. I sat with the awareness that this very minute there are women all over the world giving birth. There are thousands of babies being born today into all kinds of environments, all kinds of families. All kinds of birthing are happening as I write these words. The needs are the same the world over. I now feel more connected and part of something larger than myself and my personal situation, something more meaningful than consumer culture or, for that matter, any nationalistic culture. I feel connected to the web of life, of birth and death. I feel a part of the world and as if my tiny thread is really connected to others. By me doing the work that I do, I can affect others and the ripple will slowly spread out.

Wednesday 28th April

The potato plants were ready to be earthed up at the allotment so I drew the soil around them. I like to imagine the warm and dark environment in which they like to birth.

Then I checked the peas who like the open air and sunlight around them in order to flower and give birth to their pea pods. The tender salad leaves and radishes are rushing to grow and soak up the spring sunlight. More tender seedlings are hardening off little by little. I know that with the right care in these early days they will grow into big strong plants with delicious bounty for my table.

These plants are as alive as me in their capacity to grow and reproduce as well as to respond to changes in the internal and external environment. We are linked in our desire for life.

I began to think of the symbiotic relationship that exists between plants and humans. How I breathe out carbon dioxide, which is what they need to breathe in. How they breathe out oxygen, which is what I need to breathe in. We exist together and need each other to survive. I feel gratitude for this simple fact of nature ~ our common carbon and water-based life share this planet of blue and green.

Do plants or animals need assistance in how to live or birth? I saw that some blue tits have taken up residence in the birdhouse on the side of the apple tree. They keep flying back and forth with bits of plant material to build their nest inside. Are they conscious of the primal urge they follow to reproduce and rear their young? Do they wonder if there is life after death or if their tiny body holds a soul?

I sat in the shed and drank my tea, just watching the birds in their busy quest. Their heads are so small I doubt there is much space for any thoughts apart from daily survival and procreation.

Thursday 29th April

The gallery had taken away some of my photos of the balanced stones last week. I went in today and saw how they'd had them enlarged and framed. It was amazing to see them on a grand scale, the colours and different textures really standing out in a way I hadn't been able to see on my computer screen. I love that the gallery is taking care of all of this now. I have so much more time free to focus on creating art as well as studying to be a Doula.

I feel like I am swimming along with the direction of the river now instead of struggling against the flow. Everything is fitting itself into place and I no longer need to place so much effort on getting things done, they just happen.

I am not interested in being a big seller in the art world. Selling enough to be able to live comfortably is a blessing in itself. And what a surprise it was to find that my father had been the one responsible, in a coincidental way, for making that happen. I feel a lot of gratitude for how life has been going my way. Through the ups and downs, I have been learning a lot. It is not always easy and I still have doubts and worries to deal with.

Tonight I met with Anna and Roy for the third time at their home. They, too, had been investigating birth culture as well as their personal birth stories. As I sat and listened to them share, I had to remind myself to stay present. My mind kept drifting off into daydreams about the birth and not really focusing on what was being said. I was so lost in my head and not in my body that I couldn't hear what was going on. I had to really concentrate. When I did, I heard Roy describing his birth, as much as he knew, and young childhood.

Then I realized why I was having a hard time hearing. His birth had been very traumatic for both him and his mother. They had been separated directly after birth because he was rushed into an incubator and stayed there for many weeks before she was allowed to take him home again.

His mother was then very busy with her four other rowdy kids. Roy remembered feeling like a burden, being left to sit on the side-lines while his older brothers and sisters played rough-and-tumble. He had been small with a slight build until he reached puberty.

Then he had shot up and bulked out by combining gym workouts with heavy calorie intake. He had been the weedy kid at school before that, the sick one, the one who sat out PE every week. This had made him want to fight and to stand up and be noticed.

As he spoke, I felt the hairs rising on the back of my neck. This is going to be interesting having such a strong personality in the birthing room, I thought to myself. Was he going to be able to sit quietly while Anna took the limelight during labour? His needs would become secondary to hers during the birth as well as in the weeks following, living with a new baby. His role in the house was going to change. Was he aware and was he ready?

Anna took up the speaking space with her own story. She had been dancing since she was tiny. Her mother had given her the desire to succeed and pushed her through her ballet grading, on and on, up and up. Weekly practice became bi-weekly practice, which then became daily practice. Was this her desire or her mother's? It was hard to tell, she seemed to want what her mother wanted. Her mother had also been a dancer when she was younger and loved the whole world of dance and shows.

Gently, I guided her back to talk about her birth as I felt we could have spent hours talking about dance. The words she had been saying sounded old and well used, like a favourite jumper. I was looking for the deeper layer, the imprinting layer that lies beneath the day-to-day activities.

Anna then spoke about her own birth story. As far as she knew, it had been a natural, drug-free hospital birth. Her father had been there. She was a first child, much loved and waited for. Labour had slowed down when her mother had gotten to the hospital and, instead of accepting the drugs offered, her mother had chosen to wait. She waited a night and a day and Anna made her appearance the next evening. They went home the following day. Her mother had problems breastfeeding and, after giving it a try, she was told to give a bottle as baby was losing weight. The bottle seemed to work so breastfeeding was forgotten.

I had assumed that Anna was going to breastfeed after her natural home birth, but after hearing this, I realized I had never asked her. So I did. She said she would like to breastfeed, knowing that it was the best thing for the baby, but also knew that the bottle would be okay as well, since she had grown up on it herself.

After they had both shared their stories, I led them through some relaxation exercises. The sharing had been emotional and a lot of old dust had been stirred.

We practiced deep breathing and used positive visualisation. It helped all of us to let go of the strong emotions that had been uncovered while talking about personal experiences. The birthing time was nearing for them. I had wanted to talk more in detail about our roles during and after the birth, but that was going to have to wait for our next meeting. I hope there will be enough time. I can feel the clock ticking. I told them to think about their birth plan and that we'd discuss it more next week. This structure feels like it is helping to set us up for the imminent birth.

After tonight's sharing, however, I am worried about how Roy is going to be when we get into the high energy of the birthing environment. I also learned more about Anna and her personal relationship with breastfeeding. This made me realize that assumptions can be misleading.

Friday 30th April

I have been drinking more herbal tea since my trip to the community with Hilary. Some taste good while others have a medicinal taste that sticks in my throat. I shared some with Angelica, who wanted to try them. The ones I had found too strong, she enjoyed. Maybe that's because she is lactating?

Hilary has also been drinking more herbal tea, she told me, when I went over for afternoon tea today. On this occasion, we were drinking Earl Grey out of porcelain cups. Her baking afternoon had been a success and the spread on the table was taste-bud boggling: macaroons, lemon drizzle cake, shortbread and tea cake. I never bake so this was a treat.

She was interested to hear about the reunion with my father. I told her about his flame red hair, his gentle face and kindly manner. I am still surprised that such a man could have married my mother, who seems to be so stiff and full of anger. But as Hilary pointed out, maybe she wasn't always that way.

Birth trauma combined with the disappearance of a mentally unstable husband probably took its toll. Along with being a single mother in a generation in which that was not the norm, not accepted as it is today.

Did she have enough support while raising us to be able to look after herself and her own needs? I didn't think so. She never seemed open to accepting help or sharing her feelings. To be needy was a sign of weakness in her eyes and she criticized anyone who went around begging for help.

I learned this from her unconsciously and spent most of my life pretending that I could cope. I insisted I could do everything alone and was not one of those people that needed help. People used to comment on how strong I was, how independent and capable. Really I needed love and care as much as the next person. I never fully realized that until last month when I had my breakdown (or maybe it was actually my break through?) after Anne-Marie's birth. Now I think of myself before and feel like I could have done so much more had I had the support that I needed. But what is past is past and I now know what I did not then.

Angelica and Nick continue to be caring and loving to their daughter's fairy godmother. They often pop in when they are passing, not for anything in particular but just to spend some time. She bakes extra bread and brings me a loaf, knowing I'll never bake one myself. It's these little things that remind me how much I am loved. And in turn I show them my love by sharing surplus from the allotment and helping them around the house. I love taking Valentina for a walk round the park or into town a couple of times a week to give her parents some time alone. But most importantly, I am there whenever they need an ear to listen to them, as they are for me.

~ May ~

Saturday 1st May

Today is Beltane, according to the old pagan calendar. It is the day that marks the beginning of spring.

I spent the day with Anna, her close female friends and relatives, as they had a baby blessing. They called it a Blessingway ceremony. I had not heard of one before. The baby showers I had been to in the past were more about what presents people had brought for the new baby than anything sacred.

This one was quite different and began with an air of mystery. We had all been asked to bring a special bead and a length of coloured wool with us. Everyone would also bring a plate of food to share.

It wasn't the serious event I had imagined when her best friend Gail had invited me. She had said that no bad birth stories were allowed, not that I would have told any.

'It is about having a celebration for the coming birth,' Gail had said.

Later on, I understood why I had been specifically asked not to tell bad birth stories. The Blessingway was about intentionally creating a safe space to share and be ourselves without bringing in any negative influences from outside. There were fresh flowers and ripe fruit everywhere to set the scene of abundance.

We began by reading some blessings that Anna had chosen, and others that her friends had brought. It was a bit awkward at first. We didn't know if we were supposed to be serious or having fun. But as we settled down and listened to the words that were being read, the walls around us seemed to disappear and we were transported to a place far out of time. What was happening was something older than the walls, older than us. The words spoke to the blood running in our veins, the beating of our hearts. We were somehow connecting in with something bigger than just our little circle.

The blessings were a patchwork of readings around pregnancy, birth and being a mother, as well as other more sexual readings about the forgotten power of women.

Anna was then given a foot bath in scented water. We tore petals off roses and threw them into the basin of warm water and over her head, covering the room in pink and red splashes of colour.

We massaged her hands, her feet and her swollen belly, painting it afterwards with henna in swirling designs. We strung the beads we had each brought onto a string and she wore it around her neck to remind her of her connection to each of us. The different colours and sizes of the beads contrasted. Each bead held a different story of who had threaded it there. My offering had been a shell taken from the beach and sanded down to show the spiral hidden within. Lots of other beads were ocean related: a jade dolphin from Gail, a pearl in the shape of a heart, a blue bead with flashes of gold inside. There was one that stood out from all the rest. It was from a friend that had unfortunately not been able to come but had posted her bead to be included on the string. It was in the shape of an egg with a tiny baby carved inside and we all marvelled at the intricate design.

Then we sat in a circle with Anna like a queen in the centre. Each of us held onto the end of the thread we had brought and passed the other end around the circle.

What resulted was a giant spider's web of colours weaving around and between us. We were laughing at the chaos of the intertwining threads. Then someone, maybe Gail began singing a song and, one by one, we joined in until everyone was singing.

'From women we were born into this circle.
From women we were born unto the earth.'

Harmonies were weaving in and out, high voices mixed with low. Someone started singing from the first line again just as we had begun the second line and a round began. It was exhilarating to hear our voices lifting to the sky as we wove our threads. We were joined in song, joined by the colourful weave, united by our bond to this woman who is soon to become a mother.

Though I had not met most of these women before, I felt connected to them physically by the thread and symbolically by singing and feeling our essential feminine nature.

A pair of scissors was passed around and we cut the thread that surrounded us and tied a section of each colour around our wrists. The idea was that we would wear these until Anna went into labour. As soon as we heard that her labour had begun, each of us would cut the threads and be thinking of Anna and the baby until we heard that the baby had been born safely.

We moved onto eating the food that had been brought to share and spent a long time chatting and enjoying Anna's beautiful home. Gail came around with a pen and paper to make a food train for the days after the birth. All her friends signed up to deliver Anna a meal, letting her and Roy relax and enjoy the early days with their new-born instead of thinking about feeding themselves. It also meant that they had an excuse to come over and see the new baby.

I feel like I am part of creating a new tradition, a new birth culture. Today confirmed that. This ceremony transcended the mundane and disconnected society. It made me feel part of a sisterhood of women supporting women. We finished the day with a chant that held the safe space for us before we each went our separate ways.

'In this circle No Fear
In this circle Deep Peace
In this circle Great Happiness
In this circle Safety.'

The memory of today will stay within me for a long time to come. I have never been religious or spiritual in any way other than my own. But today touched a deep part of me and brought me into a sacred, safe space with other women who now feel as close as sisters to me.

This Blessingway ceremony felt not only like it was soul food for Anna, on her journey of initiation, but a blessing for all of those lucky enough to be witness to her transformation from maiden to mother.

I was so moved. I suggested that it would be wonderful to do this more often, not only with pregnant women but with mothers, grandmothers and women in general. To spend time together being women. Everyone agreed with my idea. As this seed has now taken root inside me, I shall see where its fruit grows.

Sunday 2nd May

We have moved into May and it feels unusually warm these days. The allotment needs watering more than usual and the water butts are nearly empty. Still my work is paying off with cut-and-come-again salad leaves ready for eating. There is also so much rhubarb that I have been sharing it around with everyone that I know. Is it possible to eat too much rhubarb crumble and pie and jam and compote?

The carrot seedlings were growing in such profusion, I had to thin them out. But I had to be careful of the carrot fly, whose nose is alerted to the presence of juicy carrots at thinning time. I watered the seedlings first in an attempt to keep the smell down. They can smell a carrot growing from a mile away! Last year was a disaster with most of the carrots becoming food for maggots. The companion planting idea with rows of onions and garlic may ward off the little vampires by confusing their noses. Taking no chances I also took all the discarded carrot seedlings off the allotment site. I took them to the compost pile that Angelica has in her back garden rather than leaving them lying around close to the remaining plants. She doesn't grow any carrots, so the flies won't bother her even if they come.

The warm weather has brought out a lot of fair weather allotmenteers and the place was full. I love it during the empty wintry days when I have the place to myself but also enjoy it when the place is full and buzzing with life. There are lots of families here and many young children are running around. As there is a no-car policy on site, it's a pretty safe space: if you don't mind the other everyday dangers of tools, tripwires of string and netting around the place.

One of my neighbours along the way grows the most amazing flowers on his patch. Not a single vegetable except potatoes and cabbage, says that all he eats is meat and potatoes with a bit of green now and then. But he does grow flowers, hundreds of them. It is an ocean of colour, a rainbow on the earth.

He used to complain about children. They longed to touch and smell his prize flowers. He put up netting, not against the pigeons like the rest of us but against the children. That was before he became a grandfather.

Last year I saw how his little granddaughter had softened his heart. He planted a special area just for her, although, of course, the other kids love it, too. There are colourful wild flowers for them to touch and smell, with different textures of grasses as well. Also, he built a bug hotel of old pots, sacking, tubes and old bricks. The kids come along with their catching pots and investigate the creepy crawlies they can capture for an afternoon's investigation.

His prize flowers still bloom beautifully and now the glow that comes from his face is lit up all the more by sharing this little corner with such eager budding gardeners. It is nice to see his crinkly edges softening by allowing love to creep into his life.

I sat outside the shed with a book and my flask after spending the morning working on inter-cropping my patch to maximize space. This was in addition to the regular work of weeding and watering, of course. The warm sun made me drowsy. I felt so relaxed and at ease, like it was honey for my soul.

I also saw Hilary today and shared with her my idea of having a women's circle. She offered her front room as a venue. With its large ceilings, beautiful view and roomy sofas, it would be perfect, I agreed. She said it would bring fresh life into her house. As long as no one minded the two dogs that lived there. I assumed that no one would mind the two dogs, they were very friendly. Using her place seemed like a great idea. I thanked her for the offer. The seed of the idea is beginning to grow quickly.

Monday 3rd May

Today I met a woman who had what she called an 'ecstatic' birth. She laughed and blushed a little when she said she felt amazing as she was bearing down, birthing her baby.

We met at a drop-in group for new mums, where I had gone with Angelica and Valentina. Her little girl was two months old. This woman told us how she had decided to give birth in a birth centre not far away. She felt that her home was not ideal and hospital was too sterile for her. She had been left alone with her husband for most of early labour after they put a 'private ~ please knock' notice on the door. Inside, they had tried the age-old labour-inducing effects of nipple stimulation and orgasm to bring on contractions.

As she talked, I realized that she had planned this event in as much detail as some people planned their weddings, down to small details like the colour of the pillows she took in with her. Her wish list for birth included fresh lilies and red roses, along with photos of her wedding day and honeymoon. I was reminded of Gail's warning about 'no negative birth stories' for during her pregnancy she had literally flooded herself with positive stories about birth. Her house became a shrine to birthing goddesses, filled with statues and pictures on the wall as she prepared for what she called 'The day I become a Mother.'

Her story was amazing and we listened avidly. She was so passionate and eager to share with us. Apparently many people didn't even want to listen to a good birth story, believe it or not. Other people couldn't bear to hear it as it made them feel bad about their own less-than-desirable experiences. They really couldn't believe that something like giving birth could be a positive, even pleasurable, experience.

It's true, we have been conditioned to be more interested when things go wrong that when things go right. How do we respond to hearing amazingly positive stories that go against everything else we have been told? Do we feel disbelief and criticism or encouragement and empowerment?

Her own mother was an extraordinary lady in her own right. This probably had something to do with how this woman felt so empowered. She told us how her mother had bought her flowers and took her out to dinner the day her periods started when she was twelve. She actually felt good to be menstruating and to become a grown woman.

I thought back to the day I began to bleed. My mother had grumbled about the extra costs and dragged me to the shops to buy some sanitary pads. All to my utter embarrassment. I could tell by the look on Angelica's face that she was remembering her own experience, and I smiled to myself.

Angelica's older sister had already started her periods as she was a couple of years older. For some reason Angelica was desperate to have periods herself, thinking they were something mysterious and womanly.

One evening she burst into the dining room where her parents were entertaining guests and announced that she had started her periods, in front of the bemused crowd. Eventually it was discovered what had happened. The beetroot they'd had for dinner the night before, which makes urine turn pink, had stained her underpants. It wasn't the desired period at all! Oh, how embarrassed she had been, her face going as red as the beetroot. Oh, how we had laughed whenever she told the story, since she could see the funny side of it now.

'Knowledge is power,' this woman told us. Her name was Flora and her positive energy seemed to bubble out of her pores. 'Let us educate ourselves about the power we hold as women.'

I shared my idea about holding space for a women's circle in my friend's flat near the park. She nearly jumped into my arms, she was so excited.

'When is the first one?' she asked with delight. I looked around to see Angelica nodding and asking for details as well.

We decided to meet on Saturday morning at ten o'clock. Of course, I had to phone Hilary to check that this was a good day for her and she confirmed it was.

I'm feeling nervous now. Who is going to come? What are we going to do? What if it all goes wrong? What if I fail? Deep breath and carry on. It is going to be fine. Even if it is only Angelica, Flora, Hilary and me, it will be fine.

Tuesday 4th May

Today there was another meeting of the breast feeding group. I popped in even though I hadn't been last week. Fern, the pregnant peer supporter, was there. I wanted to invite her to come to the gathering at the weekend. She looked a little uncertain as I explained that it was a women's circle.

'But what's it about?' she asked hesitantly.

I assured her that it was an informal group, not only for mothers but also pregnant women and even childless women like myself.

'I want to create a safe space for women to share,' I said, 'regardless of age or number of children.' She asked if she could bring a friend and I said of course she could. Hilary's front room can comfortably hold ten women or so.

I decided to do some research at home to determine what to do on Saturday. After all, it is only four days away. It does feel informal but I also want to make it special. Otherwise I know we'll just sit around and chat. I want to create an agenda for the first meeting, to guide the vision I have of creating a safe and sacred place.

Firstly, I realized that some kind of guideline needs to be in place. What is important? To create safe space confidentiality is paramount and this is built by trust. What is said in the group stays in the group.

It also feels important that we practice some of the listening skills I learned on my Doula course. To listen without interrupting, without offering advice or suggestions but just listening and being present with what the other person is sharing. What a gift that is, to speak while being heard. Not to be judged, just listened to.

I have felt how power can come through the spoken word as we release the thoughts from the cage of our heads to fly free. I felt it when I opened my heart to speak in the opening circle of the Doula training weekend, when I spoke about what it was like to be at Valentina's birth. The power was like a whooshing feeling as I felt the words take flight. I had been nervous but decided to trust myself to speak my truth and it was healing knowing that it had been heard.

When I listen to others with my whole being, not thinking of what I am going to say when my turn to speak comes around, I am freed from introspection. It is liberating to escape from my own head and to be there completely for someone else. This way it is also possible to be able to give something precious to the speaker; my undivided attention.

I also trust that when my turn comes to speak, I will be present within myself to know my own truth and allow its expression.

Some circles use a talking stick or stone that the speaker holds while talking. When you have this object you can talk, when you don't have it you remain quiet. Having experienced the magical feeling of being listened to completely, I wish to give the same gift to others.

It also feels important that we sit in a circle. No backs turned and all faces can be seen. Everyone is equally important and welcomed. There is no hierarchy or leader, only a continuous circle of loving support.

Another guideline that could be useful is that we all speak from personal experience, not someone else's. This means the truth is direct and first-hand. We can only really know something if we, ourselves, have experienced it. Regurgitating some-one else's story along with their thoughts and feelings is not our truth but someone else's. Let us leave their stories for them to tell.

After sharing the guidelines with the group comes the agenda. This could begin, I thought to myself, by opening the circle and welcoming everybody. It wasn't always easy to make time and space to nourish ourselves as women so I wanted to honour the fact that everyone had made an effort to come. Lighting a centre candle would be a nice way to focus the energy.

Introductions would be made. We could use the talking object around the circle. Saying why we are here and what hopes and fears we have about being in a women's circle. As a group we would need to define our purpose. My purpose is to create support and a safe listening space specifically for birth and mothers but also for women to be women. Does everyone agree? I would then ask whether this mirrors their own purpose. Is there anything else we could add to that?

Maybe we could think of a name to claim the group as our own.

Then I'd like us all to agree on what we are going to do, when and how often to meet. I feel that two hours is ample time for sharing, but maybe more or less is better for others. I must remember to check in with Hilary to see how she is feeling about continuing to host.

At this point, we would probably need a break for tea, cake and fruit. Not a long break from the circle, perhaps only ten minutes. After which we would come back together to close our circle and finish. A prayer or blessing or something to read would be a good way to finish. I will keep my ears open for something appropriate. Finally, by extinguishing the candle, the circle would be symbolically closed until the next time.

Writing this has gotten me excited about the whole idea, but also nervous. What if I can't get the atmosphere quite right and it becomes too serious and heavy? Or what if everyone laughs and can't concentrate?

Wednesday 5th May

It has nearly been two weeks since I saw my father. I haven't phoned him as things have been busy here.

I also needed time to process how I have been feeling after seeing him. He hasn't called either. Maybe because he also needs to process or maybe he is giving me my space. It has been an intense time for both of us. Either way, having the time and space not to think but to feel things through has been good.

I have been doing a lot of walking these past few days, amongst the meetings and planning that has been happening. I find my best ideas often come when I am walking. Things I am working on in my head seem to find their solution under the open sky. It is liberating to stop thinking, to walk and feel the wind on my face. To watch the birds flying and be aware of what is happening out and about in the world calms my mind. I feel calm and clear returning from the cliff tops or river side.

I come back to the workshop and put myself into painting or playing with the images I have created. It's funny but I find that when I concentrate less, I more get done. It's paradoxical but I believe that once I create the internal space, the outer space reflects this. There is more room to manoeuvre and it all sorts itself out.

So this afternoon I decided to call him. I wanted to ask him if his offer for me to come and visit was still open. Maybe a day trip would be a good idea. I haven't told my brother or mother about his reappearance in my life yet. I haven't spoken to either of them in weeks so it hasn't been difficult not to tell. If I can see where he lives then the whole thing might feel more real. He could be telling my anything. I guess part of me still cannot believe him. Is the story he told me about himself true? If I could see his house with my own eyes, perhaps I could truly believe it. I want to believe, I really do. I am aware, however, that part of me is hanging back.

So I called his number and a woman with a strange accent answered the phone. Who was she?

I asked for Ben, there was a pause, she asked my name, another pause, and she told me to wait. After a while he came to the phone, sounding happy and glad to hear from me.

'Who was that woman?' I tried to ask innocently but I could hear the emotion in my voice as the words cracked and dribbled into the phone. He had told me he lived alone and had no relatives. Had he been lying? Why was I so suspicious? I guess I had this image painted in my head of him living all alone in a huge flat. In my mind I saw a lonely man with only his computer for company as he tapped out his writing and looked at my solitary painting on the wall. It was a rather morose image, I realized now, as he laughed.

'That?' he asked. 'That was just Amelia; you'll have to meet her. When are you coming? Are you still coming for a visit?'

Could this man read my mind or was he trying to cover something up? Maybe he had a whole new family he had not wanted to tell me about until I got over the shock of meeting him for the first time. Maybe I had lots of step-brothers and sisters and a step-mum and....

'So?' the voice in the receiver asked and I jumped.

I had been caught up in the mental daydream of a whole imaginary family. I realized that I had not been listening to a single word he had been saying.

'Err, sorry can you repeat that last bit?' I mumbled, ashamed that I had so easily been side-tracked by an imaginary dimension.

He told me that some people at the magazine had found out that the artist he had written about in his column was his long-lost daughter. They wanted to run a story about it. They said it was like a real life soap opera and people would love to share in our happiness.

He wasn't convinced about the idea, being a private kind of person. But that was what Amelia was doing there, apparently. She was his boss and had personally come over to his house to approach him with the idea about running a story on us. He had a call on his mobile from someone he was writing about and had gone onto the balcony to talk when I had rung on the land line. So she had just grabbed it. The strange accent was because she was from Portugal.

'But do not be fooled,' he joked. 'This one has a razor sharp mind and it works just as well in English as in any other language.'

He laughed and I could hear her laughter in the background. She was obviously listening in on our conversation. I felt uncomfortable, told him I'd call back later and put the phone down. I sat looking out of the window for a while before grabbing my coat and heading to the beach.

Hilary was sitting on a bench at the end of my road as if she had been waiting for me.

'You've come,' she said and stood up. 'Come along.'

'What? Where?' I felt confused. Had she been waiting for me?

There was no time for questions. I followed her, trying to keep up as she beetled along. She led me through the park, down the embankment and onto the beach. We walked towards the row of houses that ran parallel to the beach and stopped outside one of them. She knocked on the door, which was answered by a man, who I guessed was a little older than me, with clear blue eyes.

'Oh, hi Hilary, is this her?' he asked, as he gave her a peck on the cheek and looked over her shoulder at me.

'Yes, this is the one,' Hilary replied as she disappeared inside.

'I'm sorry, should I know who you are?' I asked this strange man as he stood on his doorstep smiling at me.

'Me? Oh no, I'm nobody special,' he laughed again. His voice sounded like a stream running over stones, light and happy.

I felt most disturbed. What was going on? I felt like Hilary was being very mysterious and I wasn't sure I liked it. Especially after the odd phone conversation that had just happened with Ben. Hilary popped her head out of the front door like a meerkat out of its hole.

'Are you coming in or are you going to stand there all day?'

'Oh right, yes,' the man said as he beckoned for me to follow him inside.

'Joy, this is James.' Finally, we were introduced. 'He has been my friend for the past few years. Ever since I found out he knew how to cast a line. He always brings me fresh fish, when he catches any extra.' She nudged him in the ribs and cocked her head as if to show that this fish had been a bit thin on the ground recently.

She continued, 'I have been telling him a bit about you recently, and he wondered if you would like to go out on his boat for a trip.'

She nudged him again.

'Yes,' he said, still smiling. 'Hilary tells me how much you love the sea. We thought you might like to see how the land looks from out there.'

I looked from her face to his and saw only gentle kindness in both of them. I let out a breath and sighed. This was obviously a conspiracy although I could not divine the purpose of it at that point in time.

'I would love to go out on a boat, thank you. But why couldn't you just have told me earlier?' I looked at Hilary, who winked at me.

'You might have said no. Now that you're here, it's halfway to being done,' she replied with the air of someone who knew me almost too well already. She was right. I probably would have said no.

They obviously had this whole scheme set up for some reason and they were not going to tell me now. So again I said yes and then we were off. I didn't realize it but they meant to go out on a boat right then and there.

Hilary said goodbye and winked again. Was there something in her eye?

James and I walked to the harbour. He led me to a small wooden boat, painted green, yellow and red. I felt like I was in a picture book.

We chugged out and before I knew it we were on the open sea. Of course I had been out at sea before, on cruises and occasionally in a kayak with a friend but this afternoon was special. The light was amazing, the clouds were bubbling away on the horizon but above us it was clear blue. I felt entranced.

We motored on along the coast, past familiar landscapes. We passed the next bay, then the next. James tapped me on the shoulder, breaking the spell.

He pointed something out to me.

'Over there,' he shouted over the noise of the engine.

I looked and caught my breath. The rocks of the cliff formed what looked like a woman reclining. The grassy cliff tops were her green hair spread out behind her. Her arms, spread wide, were made of stone. Her breasts were lumps of earth. The mound between her legs sprouted another grassy clump of green perched halfway down the cliff. There in the centre of her being was a perfectly rounded bulge like the belly of an eight month pregnant woman. She was magnificent and I was in awe.

I turned to James, who smiled at me. 'Quite something isn't she?' he said. I nodded.

Now I understood why Hilary had set this little sea trip up. Her secrecy had served for the marvel and magic of this moment. I felt deep gratitude to her and also to James who had obviously shared his discovery with her. I could just imagine them planning this little scheme. But how had she known I was going to be leaving my house right when I did? How long had she been sitting there waiting on the off-chance I would come along? These questions would have to wait for another time. Right now I turned and looked, soaking up this beauty of nature. James cut the engine and pulled out his fishing rod.

'Time to catch some dinner,' he chuckled and turned to his work.

Luckily I had my camera with me and turned my attention to capturing the image of this bountiful earthen woman. She pulled me in. I wanted to talk to her and discuss the mysteries of life that she held in her womb. She seemed to hold the essence of creation and revelled in the divinity she possessed. I was in awe and had no idea how much time had passed until James told me it was time to head back as the daylight was beginning to fade.

We travelled back in silence, watching the seagulls flying towards the setting sun that cast golden streaks across the sky. The clouds were heavy now, with pink bellies full of the sun's last rays.

I thanked James profoundly for sharing this with me and he bowed his head to humbly accept my thanks. What other mysteries had this man seen?

I walked home quietly, listening to the sounds of the birds settling for the night in the treetops. The whole world seemed to hold its breath along with me as the silence inside me echoed along the roads. There were few cars and no one was about. It felt like the whole world was mine. I was pregnant with life bursting to be alive.

Thursday 6th May

Another week has passed and it's time for our fourth meeting. Anna and Roy were waiting for me when I arrived at their home. They were smiling and looking calm. We had a lot to talk about and I was grateful we still had time before the birth. I invited Anna over to Hilary's for our first women's circle and she said she would confirm tomorrow as she might have to be somewhere else.

We began our session and checked in with each other first and discussed how we were feeling since our last meeting. I brought up the issue of wanting to define our roles during the birth, mine and Roy's specifically.

We went through their birth plan together, which they had written based on their personal preferences. They wanted a home birth, with the baby being born in the pool, if possible. Their midwife had come over and checked out the house, saying that Anna was fine to give birth at home as long as no complications arose.

They wanted as little medical interference as possible. As they couldn't be sure which midwife from the team they would get for the delivery, they wanted me to be there throughout. I was to act as their advocate if things got difficult, and to make sure all health care professionals respected their birth plan.

The most important thing for them was not to be separated from the baby. After hearing Roy's birth story, I could sympathize with this. If something did happen and they had to transfer to hospital, my role would be to stay with Anna. If the baby had to be taken somewhere then it was Roy's role to stay with the baby. If everything went to plan, it would be a smooth labour and birth at home. This was their goal.

I checked in with Roy about how he might feel if people weren't listening to him and he was left on the side-lines. I knew I had found the trigger words as his body stiffened and he looked straight at me.

'Why would that happen?' he asked.

'I don't know,' I replied. 'It just might and we need to look at it now. Anna is going to be very busy. It is our job to make sure she feels safe enough to allow her body to take over. If she feels that you are not comfortable then maybe she won't be able to do that.'

I said it as directly as I could, being clear without being confrontational.

He sighed and sat back, Anna put her hand on his knee. He smiled at her.

'I'm sorry, my love. Do I do that to you?' He looked intently into her eyes and she smiled back.

'Sometimes,' she admitted.

'I will try to be aware and stay present for you,' he said in a very humble and sweet way. I hoped that trying would be enough. We talked about the importance of being a team during this. I felt the energy shift and it was time to move on.

We discussed the practicalities of going into labour. I wanted her to contact me as well as the midwife as soon as one of these things happens: her waters break, she has a show, she feels ill or bleeds or is in pain or if anything unusual happens.

We talked about getting the house ready as if there were going to be a party. This meant lots of extra food and drink. Towels, buckets and bags should be ready for the clean up afterwards. Blankets and baby clothes needed to be hands-reach away. The filling of the pool and any technical issues had all been resolved and it was ready to go at any moment. The clothes were ready for Anna after the birth. All mobile phones were to be kept charged and with credit. Important phone numbers were written out clearly next to the phone in case I needed to ring anyone during labour. There was a full tank of petrol in the car. The camera was charged. The music they wanted during labour and birth had been chosen. The birth plan had been printed with the birth statement at the top and a copy was stuck on the fridge. Their Birth Statement summarized the essence of what they most wanted during their birth:

'We want to welcome our baby with love and stay together at all times.'

We talked through the use of heat packs during labour for comfort measures and about whether she wanted any essential oils or homoeopathy, like arnica, to use. They had been doing perineal massage for the past few weeks on Leanne's advice and we talked about this. She had been using the birth breathing techniques during the massage as it was quite uncomfortable at the beginning but had been getting easier recently.

We also talked about the different stages of birth and what to expect. This was just a run through more than anything but I needed to check that we were on the same page. We talked of breast-feeding and the early days being about letting baby establish its rhythm, not trying to impose one.

I was still worried she would switch to a bottle at the first sign of any issue. But it was not my place to influence, only to provide information and support.

Anna is now thirty nine weeks pregnant, the birth could happen any day.

We finished by doing a positive visualisation of their birth, seeing the baby in their arms, welcoming their baby in their home. It was an emotional visit. Anna showed me some of the baby clothes they had ready, all looking so tiny. It was amazing to think that there will soon be a little person living in them.

Friday 7th May

This morning Ben phoned back. I hadn't thought about him at all since Wednesday and that odd phone conversation. It felt a little awkward and he apologised for putting me on the spot like that. He hadn't really been into the idea of making this public but Amelia was being very persuasive. I had called just as she was in the middle of trying to convince him it would be a good idea.

'To be honest Ben, I understand where she is coming from but I am not ready to go public,' I admitted.

He told me he understood and it was just an idea of hers. He had told her to cool off and if it happened, it happened, if not, no. She also loved my work and the magazine wanted to run an article on me. She thought that this would add a great human interest slant to it.

I really appreciate everything that has happened to my work since Ben bought my piece and the gallery took notice. But I didn't want to take it further, not yet.

'I'm happy with how things are,' I told him on the phone. 'I don't need to make millions. Making money is not my goal. And right now my energy is focused in another direction. I am passionate about being involved with birth, not selling paintings,' I confessed.

He said he understood but I could tell he didn't really. His life had been about making lots of money and now that he had it, he wanted to share the wealth, or the pathway to making it.

'Well,' he said, 'the offer is still there. She could make you rich.'

I laughed. 'You didn't hear me,' I said. 'I am happy with what I have.'

After I hung up, I realized the idea of going for a visit will have to wait until things have calmed down. When all this blows over and they have moved onto the next story, I will just be a bit of history, not worth making an issue over. However this evolves, I am so glad I have contacted my father, and met him in the flesh. His presence in my life will not be proclaimed the whole country over. I would want to tell my mother and brother first. For them to hear the story via a magazine would be horrible.

But I'm still not ready to tell them that I have met my father, at least not yet. Maybe I will go and visit Mother after the summer is over and tell her face-to-face. Show her the photo we took together on the beach when he came to visit. My brother would be silently angry beyond belief if he found out what Amelia wanted to do with the story of our reunion. It would not be something my private brother would want to be involved with. He tells me he is perfectly happy driving the library van around the villages. He has his little routines and any threat to that is a threat to his existence. A public profile would ruin him. I couldn't be a part of that.

So I said goodbye to my long-held dream of being a famous painter. It was the dream that got me through art school and into the workshop. It was my driving force while I was poor and painting with materials I picked up at the recycling centre.

But it has been a long time since I felt the desire to be famous. My life has evolved into seeing a bigger picture where community, good friends and the future of our planet is more important. I want to cultivate my inner growth and presence of mind. These are the riches I seek now. Money has become a tool to be used, not something to be sought after in itself.

In the afternoon, I popped into Hilary's to check in about arrangements for tomorrow's group. She smiled when she opened the door.

'So how was James?' she chuckled.

I laughed and thanked her for the most wonderful surprise. It turned out that she herself had not seen the woman in the cliff. James told her about it when bringing her some fish last week. She instantly knew that I would love to see it and told him about me. I asked why she had disappeared and not come along with us.

'My old legs are not seaworthy any more, but it gives me pleasure to see you so happy,' she replied. 'James is quite a catch himself,' she said. I found myself avoiding her eyes, which were searching my face.

'He is a gentleman,' I said, I really meant it. The man had made an impression on me, I had to admit.

'Well, you know where to find him, all alone in his house by the sea,' she made the point clear. He was single and should I wish to visit him, I would be welcome.

I changed the topic of conversation and showed her a print I had made of the wild woman of the cliffs. I gave it to her as a gift for the wonderful surprise she had prepared for me. She placed it in the middle of the mantelpiece between photos of children and grand-children.

There were delicious smells wafting from the kitchen but she wouldn't let me in to see what she was concocting. She was having an afternoon baking 'just a few little things' for tomorrow's circle.

I left, saying I would see her in the morning and walked home via the park where we had first met under the magnolia tree. Today there was another surprise waiting for me, the Handkerchief tree was blooming. The hand-length long, pure white petals were fluttering gently in the evening breeze. They caught my breath and I stood there, just like the day I met Hilary in this very park under the magnolia tree. It was only three months ago, but if feels like a lifetime. The incredible blooms look exactly like folded pocket handkerchiefs. I understand its name now.

Although officially it is called the Davidia Involucrate after the French Franciscan missionary, Père David. He was a keen naturalist who lived in China at the turn of the twentieth century. He was the first man from the western world to find the tree not Ernest Henry Wilson, as I had thought. But Père David lost his specimen on the way back to Great Britain in a shipwreck. Ernest's ship was also wrecked a few years later when he was bringing back his specimen. But Ernest managed to save his tree from the wreckage and present it to the western world. Interestingly its Latin name was of Père David, not Wilsons. History does not always favour the winners of the race.

Saturday 8th May

Our Women's Circle welcomed six women this morning ~ Hilary, Angelica, Fern, Flora, Sally and me. Valentina was also present. We met in Hilary's front room, united in our wish to create a circle of support and trust.

It is the evening now. I am sitting in my window again looking out into the darkness. The day has flown by and I feel lighter, empty in a good way.

The women's circle this morning was a success. The atmosphere was amazing. We built on the base of trust through confidentiality, active listening and personal experiences to create something wonderful.

Although I facilitated the circle, it didn't feel like I was in charge. Having outlined my idea, everyone agreed it seemed like something they wanted to be a part of. It felt like we were tapping again into something older than we were as we sat facing each other in the same way we did at the Blessingway ceremony for Anna. Women have been meeting in circle for longer than we have been sitting within walls.

We passed around a large shell from the beach as a talking piece, as each had our turn at sharing.

It was a time to nurture and inspire each other through being supportive. No one had to be anything except her true self. Our strengths were shared, our weaknesses accepted, our vulnerability heard. Each of us is unique and brought something individual to the group which made it special.

For a first meeting, it couldn't have been more successful. We all agreed to continue with the group, meeting once a week at Hilary's house. We didn't feel like it needed to have a strict agenda. Just to have a circle and a space to be heard was a blessing in itself, to be accepted just as we were.

The loose agenda I had planned worked well. We lit a candle and shared where we were in our lives. That was all really but it was so profound. We didn't find a particular name for the group so decided to just call it 'Our Women's Circle' and that claimed it as our own.

We agreed to open the space again next week if we knew of anyone else who wanted to come. After that we would close it for a while to build up the trust amongst us. Perhaps in time it would expand to include others. But it felt healthy putting boundaries on who came into our space, rather than having new faces every week that would change the dynamic.

Anna had phoned yesterday to say she couldn't make it and I felt surprisingly relaxed about her not coming. I needed to share some things about being a Doula. I talked about the responsibility of being totally present for someone else regardless of what was going on in my own life. If she had been there I might have guarded my words and been overly aware of what effect my sharing might have had on our relationship. I needed a safe space to be me ~ not a Doula, not an artist, just me. I also needed support and the space to be able to show my vulnerability, as well as my strength as a woman.

I've seen huge changes in my life these past weeks: meeting my father, becoming a Doula, turning away from being a fashionable artist in a glossy magazine. I have been learning how to listen to the song of my own heart and that takes courage.

I am still in need of nurturing and this circle gave me so much. To share my story without limit, without having anyone tell me what to do or how to fix it, with attentive listening and open hearts. I was able to hear my own truth come out.

Fern, the peer supporter, came up to me afterwards. Her belly was poking out from under her loose fitting shirt.

'I want to talk to you one day about being my Doula,' she said.

I felt honoured to be approached, as tentative as the enquiry was. Especially after the deep sharing I had done about my own fears surrounding being a birth companion. Maybe all she needed was someone to talk to about her birth plans or maybe I would end up being with her throughout the birth. We left the idea open to develop naturally. There was no sense of urgency about it, both of us feeling relaxed and comfortable sharing the sacred space we had created together. We would talk more next week.

Sunday 9th May

Today was calm and quiet. I am aware that I have been on call for Anna for the last two weeks, secretly hoping we would have enough time to cover everything I wanted to in our antenatal meetings. Luckily the baby hasn't come early and all is well.

Tomorrow is the calculated due date and I am still feeling relaxed about the whole thing. I hadn't even packed my Doula bag until this morning when I thought, I should do that. So I packed it straight after breakfast.

I have a copy of their birth plan in my bag as well as a change of clothes and toiletries. I also have a good book with suggestions for comfort measures should I need some extra ideas during labour. I have not turned off my phone, just in case. I plan on walking to their house as it is only ten minutes away.

The allotment is blooming and bursting at the seams. I am eating salad so fresh it hardly knows it has been picked before it is washed and served on my plate. Crunchy radishes and tender young carrots along with mixed spicy leaves and fresh herbs.

I also had my very first crop of peas. So sweet they melted on my tongue. All these delicate tastes mix and combine to create a plate of the joys of spring. My strawberry patch was pampered this week, with a bed of fresh straw for the berries to rest upon. As with the asparagus patch, I love to lavish such luxury upon them knowing that, in time, it will be paid off with lush produce. It is about preparing today for the delicacies of tomorrow.

As I think again about Anna and Roy, I feel like yesterday has set me up beautifully to be more present for them. Having been listened to in the circle, I am more available mentally to listen to someone else.

Today I sat in my flat, enjoying the peace of looking out to sea. I remembered the sea trip I took with James on Wednesday, the beautiful goddess of the cliffs with her grassy green hair. I also remembered his face as he stood peacefully looking out to sea, and the memory took me by surprise. I found myself thinking of his strong arms and kind eyes, things I hadn't even registered while we were out on the sea together. But now his image returned and I found myself wondering if I would see him again.

There was housework to be done and as I cleaned I felt myself cleansing and letting go of old aches. I let go of any expectations I was having about my father. He was not like my grandpa. I realized I had unconsciously put them together as though made of the same clay. I guess it was because Grandpa had been a father figure for me and so I automatically assumed that my father would be able to fill those boots. But my father is not that kind of person, his values are different. Throughout his life he has worked hard to become wealthy and finds it difficult to understand how anyone would not want the same.

As I watered the plants up at the allotment yesterday afternoon, I remembered Grandpa's rough hands guiding mine to show me where to weed. He taught me how many stones to pick out of the soil and how many to leave. He showed me how to choose the strongest seedlings and thin out the weakest, what time of day to water and what time of day to rest.

After finishing the housework, I lay on the sofa and read all afternoon. I am feeling more at ease with whatever may come in the next few days. It is amazing, really, looking back to how I felt just seven weeks ago when Anne-Marie went into labour. I see now just how far I have come with all this. How much more supported and prepared I feel this time around, and also how much less pressured.

In our meetings together we have covered a lot of groundwork, from discussing personal experiences and beliefs to looking at how to work together as a team. We have discussed our roles during and after birth and prepared ourselves in case of a transfer to hospital. We have built up trust and respect during our meetings together. I have learned more about how to step in when needed and also when to step out again. I hope I am able to do this when things get more intense around the birthing time.

Monday 10th May

Another D-day has come and gone but I haven't heard a whisper. All quiet. I didn't phone remembering I had told them how few babies come on their due date. In light of this, they decided to book a night out for dinner together, a final date before they become three.

I have been thinking of them so much these past weeks, more and more in the last few days. It is interesting being so intimately involved with them during this period of time. They feel close right now. But will what happens during the birth affect that? What will happen if the birth doesn't turn out like they planned? Will I feel responsible?

I had a conversation with Leanne on the phone this afternoon. I called to talk about the birth and share some fears with her. She listened and allowed me to let the doubts clear out of my head. Afterwards I felt so much better. She didn't offer any advice just let me hear my own fears. They didn't need to be soothed. Later we talked through the birth plan and ran through some comfort measures to use if needed. She reminded me that I was not responsible for the outcome of the birth. My role was to be a companion for the journey.

This evening I had dinner with Marilyn. She knew I was on call and could cancel at any moment but it was lovely to have something planned so that I wasn't sitting at home waiting. She came over and I cooked for her. We didn't talk much about the approaching birth but about painting, galleries and the art world. It was a relief to switch off for a while and talk about something other than birthing, surprisingly enough.

She wanted to hear all about Amelia and her offer. When I explained the whole situation she understood why I had refused to become another article in that magazine.

Marilyn paints for the sheer love of it. Her pieces sell at high prices but she also puts some of them into free galleries for everyone to enjoy. Her bright vibrant style brings colour and a feeling of gaiety and hope to any room.

We discussed her upcoming trip to Rio de Janeiro where she was hoping to get more inspiration as well as improve her Portuguese. She is well-travelled, often taking trips abroad on painting holidays in the French hills or Portuguese coast.

I travelled with her through her eyes, listening to the descriptions of light and colour. I saw how the bright light of foreign climes influenced her work and made her colours so bright. Our little town here has good light, something that brings many artists from around the country to come and spend time here. It certainly drew me in like a magnet.

But it was dull when compared to other more exotic places. Maybe one day I will travel to take in some of the world and bring back fresh inspiration, I thought. But right now, I realise that I have been travelling to the furthest reaches of myself, discovering lost inner landscapes and unravelling mysteries within. It has been like travelling to another country, but the country is me.

Tuesday 11th May

I was up on the allotment when Anna phoned this afternoon. She'd had a show. It indicated that labour could be starting soon. But she had not had any contractions yet. Her lower back ached a bit and she was keeping busy by cooking and cleaning out the kitchen cupboards. I told her to carry on and phone me if anything changed. I finished up what I was doing and came home to prepare myself to go over to her house later. She was fine with Roy, for the moment. It might still be a long time coming, so it would be best to continue with the day.

The cats wouldn't leave me alone when I got home. They wound themselves around my legs and sat on my lap every time I sat down. Were they trying to tell me something?

Anna phoned again and as soon as I answered, I could tell by her voice that something was happening. She wasn't making a lot of sense on the phone. She was talking about totally unrelated things then stopping mid-sentence to take a deep breath. I asked to speak to Roy, who sounded fine but asked when I was coming over. I told him to stay with Anna, to remind her that the baby was coming and to practice some of the breathing techniques we had done together.

'Oh,' he said. 'What? Do them now?' He also sounded a bit confused.

'Yes,' I said. 'This is early labour, remember your plan.'

Funny, really, that after so much planning and talking about the event it hadn't clicked for both of them that this was it.

I gently reminded him to call the midwifery team. I would be on my way soon. I made a cup of tea and decided to write this down to give them an hour to establish themselves and come to terms with the fact that labour was starting. I didn't want to rush in and take over by telling them what to do.

So this was it. I sat and did some breathing myself to prepare for the work ahead. I needed to set aside my own agenda, my own hopes and fears, to prepare to be there for whatever happens.

I remembered back to the Blessingway ceremony I was part of along with Anna's friends all those days ago. As I cut the thread that was on my wrist I mentally placed myself with Anna and the coming baby, thinking positive thoughts for their birth.

I gave Gail a quick call to let her know that labour had begun and to call the other women. I knew that they, too, would be cutting the threads on their arms to send their thoughts and prayers to Anna. They would be with us in their thoughts throughout whatever was to come.

I counted on their silent prayers to give us the strength and courage we needed now. I was sure Anna was doing the same.

Wednesday 12th May

A beautiful, healthy baby boy was welcomed into this world at six o'clock this morning. I found out later that today is actually Mayday according to the old Julian calendar, which was discarded in favour of our current Gregorian calendar in 1752. As our Blessingway ceremony had been held on first of May this felt like a happy coincidence.

I arrived at their house yesterday in the late afternoon and was shown into the bedroom, where Anna was leaning over the birth ball rocking herself gently. She didn't see me so I sat quietly until she opened her eyes and realized I was there. She reached out and I took her hand.

'I'm so glad you're here,' she smiled at me.

The bead necklace was wrapped around her other hand. Each bead held a memory of the women who were invisibly with us now.

Roy was sitting on the bed, holding a glass of water which he passed to her. We sat like this for some time. Working together through the rushes as they came, one by one, until the doorbell sounded. The midwife had arrived.

I looked at Roy, he looked at me. Who was going to answer the door? I knew it was my call, it was part of my role. But Roy got up before I could untangle my hand from Anna's. She was gripping my hand tightly, as he could plainly see. I don't think she even noticed as he slipped out of the room. I thanked him silently for his understanding. The plan needed to be flexible.

We heard voices in the hall and unfamiliar steps on the stairs. In walked a midwife I had never seen before. She was talking loudly, chatting about the difficulty parking and asking all kinds of questions. I saw Anna's body stiffen slightly as she tried to make sense of the questions that were tumbling into the quiet space we had created.

The midwife wanted to do an internal straight away to see how far along things were. Anna and Roy both looked at me. We had discussed the preference for minimum internals during early labour. It was my time to step up to my role as birth Doula.

I stood up and gently manoeuvred the midwife back down the stairs and into the kitchen. I chatted with her a little about her journey here to cover the fact that I was leading her away from the birthing mother.

When we got to the kitchen, I offered her a chair and made a cup of tea. I continued talking quietly in a subtle effort to get her to mimic me and lower the volume of her own voice. I sat down with her and pushed over the birth plan which was lying on the table. In big letters at the top, under the birth statement, it said:

'We wish to be allowed to birth quietly with as little interference as possible.'

The midwife, who was called Sarah, turned to me.

'I am only trying to do my job.' She looked hurt, like this was a personal attack against her. She ultimately had the responsibility of care and I respected her role. Internal exams were her way of knowing that things were progressing smoothly. This way any problem could be quickly identified and dealt with before complications arose.

I told her I would go upstairs and talk to them while she drank her tea and read the rest of the birth plan. She nodded and turned her attention to the biscuits I had left out on a plate.

Upstairs, things were obviously progressing. Roy was stroking Anna's back in time with her breath while she rocked with eyes closed. The contraction finished and they turned to look at me. There were questions in their eyes.

'You are doing so well,' I smiled at them both.

'I want to get into the pool,' Anna said.

I talked to them about the possibility of Sarah doing a quick internal before she got in, while Roy made sure the pool was ready. She agreed. Roy went downstairs to tell the midwife that Anna would be coming down shortly and that she could do an internal before Anna got into the pool.

While Anna and I were alone upstairs there were a few more contractions close together, and we rode the waves of them. In between the rushes, I focused on reminding her to relax and let her body go completely floppy every time she breathed out. While she breathed in, I reminded her to focus on breathing for the baby, sending energy for its journey into the world.

I don't know how long we were there but after a while she moved to stand up. I followed her lead. We walked together towards the door and down the stairs, which she did one step at a time, side-stepping. We stopped in the middle of the stairs for a contraction to pass, her head resting on my shoulder.

Downstairs, everything was ready. Sarah had laid out her things and held back from talking or questioning when we came into the room. I could feel that she now understood where we were coming from. Reading the birth plan had done its job. When I smiled at her, she nodded back.

Roy was standing next to the pool, which looked invitingly warm. Anna lay back on the sofa while Sarah pulled on her gloves and checked Anna's progress. She was pleased to say that things were moving on well and that baby was fine. She didn't say how many centimetres Anna was dilated, I later found out it was six centimetres at that point. By now it was early in the morning, but that almost seemed irrelevant. Time had flown by since I had arrived eight hours earlier. Anna was totally engrossed in herself and what was happening, as was I.

She moved into the pool and Roy got in also, sitting behind her like a human cushion. There was music playing softly and I checked to be sure the lights were dimmed.

Sarah settled herself into the sofa. I sat on the floor, ready to be active if needed but at that moment just watching Anna and Roy. They seemed to be communicating through touch alone. He stroked her back and her arms. She rocked gently with her eyes closed before flopping back into his arms. I could feel the love between them. It was almost tangible it was so strong. The room was flooded with this feeling. I was aware now that it was the love hormone: oxytocin.

Until that moment, I had never even considered having children of my own. But something about what I was witnessing opened my eyes to the other side of becoming a parent. It was an incredible bond between two people, sharing something so intimate and life-changing, forged by love and commitment. It was the transition into becoming a family, into becoming part of something bigger than themselves. They were crossing the threshold into another life. It was like nothing that I have ever witnessed. There was such raw tenderness. I felt honoured to be sharing this moment with them, and also very humbled by the strength of birth.

I offered them drinks occasionally, in-between contractions. But aside from that, I was a passive observer in awe of the surrender to the process of birth. Anna was absolutely amazing. She was inside herself, eyes closed. She swayed and danced to a rhythm only she could hear. Roy was right, there supporting her every step but without distracting her. I admired him and his quiet strength so much. The fact that he was there with her but not trying to lead her in the dance showed just how much he loved her. I knew how hard it must be for him not to try and lead her, but he was doing it and doing it so well.

Then at one point she started to cry, quietly at first then louder until she was sobbing.

'I can't do this,' she whined. 'It hurts and I want it to end. When is it going to end? I want to get out. Take me to the hospital. Get me out of here!'

Roy was alarmed. This hadn't been in the birth plan. He looked at me, eyebrows raised, and I took a deep breath. Anna had changed position and was getting louder in her protests. The midwife had sat up as well, reaching for her heartbeat monitor.

'Can't you all hear me?' Anna demanded, 'I can't do this.'

It was obvious that she was losing her rhythm. Roy looked at me. I moved over to be next to her.

'Look at me Anna,' I said.

She shook her head, stubbornly.

'Look at me,' I repeated. 'Your baby is coming, it is nearly here. Look at me.' I grabbed a piece of baby clothing that was laid out on a pile of receiving blankets next to the pool. She slowly opened her eyes and looked at what I was holding.

'There is soon going to be a baby in here,' I told her. She looked at my face then and the tears rolled down her cheeks.

'I don't know if I'm going to be any good at being a mother,' she whined. 'I don't know how to look after a baby. I'm scared.'

I took a deep breath, her fears were surfacing and that meant that labour was progressing.

She sighed as I took a deep breath in time with hers. We synchronized our breathing. I was encouraging her to take long, deep breaths to move away from the short shallow breaths that brought on more panic. We continued breathing together for a while. Her sobs ebbed away. Thankfully, it seemed like the moment of doubting was passing. I don't know what I would have done if she had continued to say she couldn't do it any-more.

Sarah had listened to the baby's heartbeat and confirmed that all was well. Then things went quiet for a while. The huge waves of contractions that had been crashing over her like waves onto a beach slowed. Roy held her like a child and told her how much he loved her. He whispered into her ear about how happy he was to be the father of their child. He told her what a wonderful mother she was going to be. He believed in her. The fear and tension left her face. She looked at me and smiled thankfully.

The tension in the room had passed like a cloud in front of the sun, which began to shine again. We all relaxed into this lull.

Then the contraction waves came back again. Anna was on all fours now, her head buried into Roy's chest. I laid hot compresses on the part of her lower back that was out of the water.

'Warmth is so soothing,' Anna had told me during one of our prenatal meetings. She had told me just what I needed to know to make this exact moment more comforting for her.

She started making different sounds, as if the air caught in the back of her throat. Sarah went out of the room to call a second midwife, who was now on her way. Suddenly there was a lot of movement in the room as preparations were made, this baby was coming soon.

Anna was not aware of any of this. She was lost in the landscape of her body. She groaned and moaned and made guttural sounds. We were all close around her now, knowing that the baby was on its way down. It wouldn't be long.

She started to push. Sarah encouraged her. Anna held onto Roy's shoulders and he kept his eyes fixed on her face, telling her how well she was doing and that the baby was coming.

Then the head was out. I could see the smooth round head under the water, covered in dark hair. It had its eyes open and was blinking!

Time seemed to stand still. Anna reached down and felt her baby's head between her legs. Then the baby turned itself and slid out into the warm water.

Sarah caught the baby just as the second midwife came in, through the unlocked door. Forward thinking had helped as we knew we wouldn't want to have to go and open the door at a critical moment.

Anna managed to turn around and the baby was placed on her chest. Roy was behind her and held them both in his arms, tears rolling down his face. He had been amazing in his role as birth partner. It was now his role to announce the sex of the baby.

'It's a boy,' he said, triumphantly.

I had been trying to take photos quietly during the labour and now took more of the new family. They were laughing and smiling and the baby was looking around at this new world he had arrived into.

The midwives checked the baby right there on Anna's chest. Satisfied, they then settled down to wait for the placenta to come. Before long, the baby began to bob its head around and move from side to side.

Anna looked up. 'What's the matter with him?' She asked quietly.

It had been a long emotional night and we were all tired. We looked at the midwives to explain what was happening.

'He is looking for your nipple,' the second midwife said. Of course!

We looked back at the baby. He was breastfeeding happily. He had attached himself to the nipple! Anna began to weep, happy tears this time. There were a couple more contractions and the placenta plopped out.

It was thoroughly inspected and her uterus was checked. All was well.

Mother and baby were tucked up in a clean warm bed with breakfast. I set to work cleaning up and emptying the pool. I was tired but elated, it had gone so well. What a blessing to be witness to such a beautiful beginning. I am going to sleep now, the adrenalin I felt from the birth is winding down and I realize I have not slept for two days.

Thursday 13th May

I debriefed with Leanne over the phone about the birth and as I finished, she congratulated me.

'On what, exactly?' I asked.

Then I realized that this second birth, along with the paperwork I had submitted last week, qualified me as a Doula. No longer a trainee, I did not need to debrief with Leanne after any more births, did not need to submit any more assignments.

But this did not mean the end of my learning. It was just the beginning, and where I went with it from here was up to me. My certificate would be in the post next week and I could now advertise my services as a qualified Doula. If I wanted to be on the national database I may have to complete other assessments for them but as far as my course with Leanne went, this was it. I feel indebted to her, having her as my personal mentor as these wonderful but difficult three months have changed me as a woman. I hope that in my work, I will be able to share some of these gifts with the women I work with.

We are all bound by the same thread of life and death, of birth and what lies beyond. I looked at the photo I had printed out of the Wild Woman of the Cliffs. She spoke to the part of me that was untamed and wild. It was the part that heard the cries of women in labour, along with the screaming of the gulls by the sea shore. Both were wild and natural, free expressions of life.

I will go over to see Anna, Roy and Ryan, their little king, later on. My role has changed but remains constant in some ways. I will continue to support their transition into parenthood, to nurture them as they find their own way. Birth is just the beginning. I talked to Roy about his role in supporting breastfeeding, the things he could do to help Anna and Ryan become an efficient team. They had their friends bringing them food for the next week, coordinated by Gail who would be going over later today with the first offering. This was a welcome addition to the widening support circle they would need in the coming days. Parenting was never a job for two people alone.

I feel good. I feel like I have made a difference not only to the lives of Anna and Roy by supporting them in their birthing but also, possibly, to the future life of their son. I thought again of what Leanne and I had talked about, how we are born affects our whole life. Our birth can set the stage for our personality and emotional life. If this was so then I had played my part for the future. Who knows what effect his birth will have on the world? Who he will grow up to be?

As a good friend once said to me, 'It takes a village to raise a child.' I am part of that village now.

Friday 14th May

It is three months today since I attended my first birth. It is also the end of the 'fourth' trimester for Angelica and Valentina, as that three month period after birth is called. Funny how I used to call her Jelly, once upon a time. After witnessing her transition into motherhood, my respect and awe of her as a woman has grown. I can still see my old friend, who often had Jelly legs, especially when we would go out drinking and partying, but she has changed. She has been surpassed by this incredible woman who has the powerful capacity to create life. She is a mother.

It has also been my first trimester of initiation into becoming a Doula. A transition that I feel is still processing and in a continuing state of development. Leanne told me that you never stop learning in this profession. Every birth teaches us something new about the power of birth, of life itself, and about ourselves.

I have become more aware of so many things. My previous life seems like a dream. I was alive but not fully living. My past had affected me so deeply and left such deep scars that I was afraid they would rip open if I dared to even look at them. They are not so scary any more. Looking deep within took me into dark scary places, and also helped healing to occur.

I feel things I could never have felt before, like compassion for my mother's own journey, her suffering and trauma. Knowledge of my father and his side to the story brought clarity to the questions that had chased me whenever I sat long enough for them to catch up. I have wept for my sister for the first time. I am more in touch with how I feel about her non-existence rather than ignoring the hole she left in our lives.

Delving into the past has validated many of my feelings and my intuition. This, together with the scientific knowledge I have gained through studying, has given me a great gift. It feels like I am standing at the edge of something quite unlike anywhere I have ever been before.

I am more aware of myself as a woman and more aware of my relationship to other women. Meeting James has also reminded me that I am a woman in a different sense of the word. I bumped into him today on the street. A wide grin appeared on his face when he saw me and I felt my mouth stretch wide in response. It was the first time I had seen him since our trip to see the 'wild woman of the cliffs' and I thanked him again for showing her to me. He then invited me out next week to visit a pebbled cove along the coast. A place only accessible by boat, he said. I am looking forward to the trip, not only to explore the coastline but also to get to know this intriguing man.

Life is stretching out in front of me, full of unexplored regions, both physical and emotional. I feel like an explorer of myself, having delved deep within to find my own truth, my own beliefs. I now have new tools at my disposal with which to continue my exploration. I realize that I was missing something in my life ~ the courage to see and accept myself just as I am. Along with this self-acceptance, self-confidence is born. These are my gifts, priceless gifts given to me by the experiences of the journey. Every experience is an opportunity.

∞ *The End* ∞

~ Author's note ~

The plant hunter Ernest Henry Wilson and his wife, Helen Ganderton, were real people living at the turn of the twentieth century. I don't know if she was an avid horticulturist, nor if she collected specimens but he most certainly did. They were only married for six months before he was sent overseas to collect trees and plants. He was employed by the Veitch brothers who were based in Exeter, Devon.

Ernest brought thousands of specimens from China to the UK, including the spectacular Handkerchief tree. This tree can be found in parks and arboretums around the country and is well worth a visit in late May.

~ Reading List ~

Heart and Hands
by Elizabeth Davies

Spiritual Midwifery
by Ina May Gaskin

Effective Birth Preparation
by Maggie Howell

The Functions of Orgasms
by Michel Odent

The Birth Partner
by Penny Simpson

Pregnancy, Childbirth and the Newborn
by Simkin, Whalley & Keppler

Birthing from Within
by Pam England

Hypnobirthing
by Marie Morgan

Natural Family Living
by Peggy O'Mara

The Red Tent
by Anita Diamant

~ Acknowledgements ~

Through the birthing of this book I have been blessed with many helping hands for which I am grateful beyond words.

The loving support and inspiration of the *Birthing Wisdom* circle in Totnes led by Olivia Seck has been priceless. I especially wish to thank Jenny Rose for her creativity and Kate for her untiring ear and support during the early days.

I wish to thank all the wonderful Midwives and Doula's at *Midwifery Today* for showing me the awe-inspiring strength and beauty that birth workers can have.

Thank you to my dear friend Becca, from *Soul Blueprint*, who put in tireless hours editing the manuscript and encouraged me endlessly.

Other people I wish to thank include Jill for her encouragement, Katinka for her passion, Lina for her explanations of the flop, Jenn butterfly for her confidence, Jane, Louise, Becca and Cristina for the solstice connection, Nicky and Dave for their support, Terri for being my early reader and giving me the push to carry on, the *Exeter Home Birth Support group* and the *Bosom Buddy Breastfeeding peer support group* in Exmouth. Also Claire Arnold for her immaculate attention to details And finally much gratitude to Rio who has been enthusiastic all the way through writing this book. I am blessed to continue sharing the journey with you.

~ About the author ~

Hazel Tree has been exploring life and writing about it since she was a young girl growing up in Devon, England. Where she developed a profound appreciation of Mother Nature.

Inspired by her own birthing experience she qualified as a Doula, a Holistic Birthing Assistant and Breastfeeding Peer Support Worker. She feels blessed to share the journey of pregnancy, birth and beyond with women from all walks of life. Hazel is also a great promoter of the importance of home in its many aspects: home birthing, home educating and home-based work.

Hazel felt drawn to write *A Doula's Journey* as a way to bring together the scientific and practical side of supporting childbirth as well as showing the emotional and intuitive journey that can happen. She is interested in childbirth as a human rights issue and from an anthropological perspective. She brings with her a wealth of wisdom and personal experience gleaned from cross-cultural immersion.

Find out more:

www.ADoulasJourney.co.uk

~About the editor~

Becca Haydon is a holistic health educator who began Soul Blueprint out of her passion to help people live healthy, fulfilled lives. With a master's degree in education and over twenty years of experience with multiple healing modalities, Becca empowers each person to access the innate wisdom of the body and soul--our soul blueprint. Through such powerful tools as Life Tracking, Numerology and ancient Yogic wisdom, we can each find our natural balance, which IS alignment with Spirit, abundance, prosperity and joy.

To set up a free thirty-minute consultation and find out how Becca's tools could benefit you, please visit her website:

www.SoulBlueprint.com

Space for notes & thoughts ...

CPSIA information can be obtained at www.ICGtesting.com
Printed in the USA
BVOW04s2238010914

364846BV00001B/1/P